They Change the Subject

Also by Douglas A. Martin

Outline of My Lover

Servicing the Salamander

My Gradual Demise & Honeysuckle

The Haiku Year (coauthor)

They Change the Subject

Douglas A. Martin

The University of Wisconsin Press
Terrace Books

The University of Wisconsin Press
1930 Monroe Street
Madison, Wisconsin 53711

www.wisc.edu/wisconsinpress/

3 Henrietta Street
London WC2E 8LU, England

1   3   5   4   2

Printed in the United States of America

Library of Congress Cataloging-in-Publication Data
Martin, Douglas A.
They change the subject / Douglas A. Martin.
    p.   cm.
ISBN 0-299-21474-5 (pbk.: alk. paper)
    1. Gay men—Fiction.   I. Title.
PS3563.A72355T47   2005
        2005008264

Terrace Books, a division of the University of Wisconsin Press,
takes its name from the Memorial Union Terrace, located at
the University of Wisconsin–Madison. Since its inception in 1907,
the Wisconsin Union has provided a venue for students, faculty,
staff, and alumni to debate art, music, politics, and the issues of the day.
It is a place where theater, music, drama, dance, outdoor activities, and
major speakers are made available to the campus and the community.
To learn more about the Union, visit www.union.wisc.edu.

For being there
while I worked through much of this material,
to BB.

"I can understand everything that hunger and poverty make you do—that's my brand of intelligence."

Marguerite Duras, "Whole Days in the Trees"

Acknowledgments

My thanks to the editors of the following journals where some of these pieces first appeared: *Dublin Review* ("They Change the Subject"), *Lit* (a different version of "A Model Love"), *Literary Review* ("An Escort"), and *Narrativity* ("21, Compositions").

License

He was the first boy I was ever really comfortable with. He said watch, if we drive around in circles long enough, some man is going to start following us. He said he could get someone to go after us, based on how we looked in the car.

His hair was like a lamb's.

Do you want to do it? he asked me.

We drove in circles around the block. We both knew this was a gay bar we were circling. It wasn't that hard to figure out.

After we'd driven around for a while and nothing happened, we hadn't seen anything, he said there was somewhere else we could go. I said OK. Then he drove us to the park.

The road that wound around the park made a bigger circle for us than the block the bar was on. If you went around enough times, you could make out the same cars doing the same thing. You could see license plates, some interiors, some of the faces in shadows.

He asked me if I wanted to pick out someone to follow. Do you want to see if we could get someone to follow us if we start following them?

Although I didn't know exactly what we were doing, I did want to be with him. We hadn't seen each other all summer. He'd decided we needed to have other friends.

I planned to pick out someone to follow by just finding a car I liked. There wasn't that much to go on.

That one.

Ugh, that guy's ugly.

Oh.

He thought we should rehearse lines. What were we going to do if someone followed us? What would we say if they stopped us?

He said we would have to go through with it, if someone did stop.

We pulled off the paved track around the park to a dirt lot. I could see myself in the passenger side rearview mirror. I was his passenger. My parents had no idea where I was, even though it was late on a school night. I could see a baseball field sprawled before us. The guy who had started following us pulled off too, up alongside us, rolled down his window and told us we should park our car over where he pointed, if we wanted to go for a ride with him.

Sure, he said. He just wanted to see what it would be like.

All right, I said. It was only acting, right? It was good practice for us.

We had our fake names ready. We had these elaborate stories all plotted out. This is who we were and where we were from. I still hadn't admitted to myself what was about to maybe actually happen, that it would be with a guy, not a girl, that this would be my first time.

We were about to reveal ourselves, he and I, to each other. I didn't want any misgivings to get in the way of that.

I think something like this could be why we had stopped being friends last summer, why he said he couldn't be friends with me anymore. He said we saw each other too much. We were getting too close to be friends, and he had hoped I'd understand. He gave me the note in the library on the last day of our junior year.

I found out later he didn't know what to do with what he had started feeling.

He had wanted to go for a drive tonight. He had just called me up out of the blue, asked me if I wanted to go for a drive with him tonight. Here we were about to get in the car with this other man now. I wanted to take with me the hairbrush I'd found on the floorboards of my friend's parents' car. We could use it as a weapon if we needed one, I joked. I pretended it didn't mean anything. My name was going to be Katch. I'd poke the guy in the eye.

I didn't know how far we were planning on going. I was told by the man to drive, drive down the highway, but to take it slow. He didn't want us to draw any undue attention to ourselves.

His head of close curls slipped into the back where the man was waiting for him. I'm in love with him. I realized that. I try to concentrate on keeping the car under fifty-five, steady.

The road rolls out black, comes back at me and then is gone.

The car I'm driving is a silver Mercedes. I've jammed the hairbrush down into one of my front pockets, and it pokes at me.

Where should I drive?

Turn onto the Interstate. Just keep driving.

His voice is like gravel on glass, as sharp and cold and insistent.

It's only a matter of minutes before there are these slurping sounds in the backseat, and I hear my friend trying not to moan, like I can't guess what's going on. It sounds a little like he's being hurt. But it's not an urgent enough sound to seem like a crisis. Just every so often, his breath pops, punctuating his breathing pattern with a sharper sigh than his normal exhaling.

He makes another primitive uuh. I keep driving as these emissions come more rapidly. I try to look into the rearview mirror to see what's happening to him but can't make out anything in the shadows of the backseat. I can see only the man bent over my friend's lap. Some lights on the road then render the slightly balding back of the man's head, his thin black hair, the side skin of his cheek glistening, shiny.

I start to cry quietly without saying anything, just keep driving. This could be happening to anyone.

Something happens that causes the man to ask me to pull over to the side of the road. He's talking to my friend. Why don't you drive now?

My friend opens the back door and I open the front, so we can change places on the shoulder of the road. The man asks us if we want to change places. The man in the back is waiting for me.

My friend asks quietly on the shoulder of the road if I'm all right.

Yeah. Is he? I don't really look at him, just at the ground, then I move down and crawl into the backseat, follow through under the man's waiting arm. My friend is someone different to me now. We are different to ourselves.

The man opens my pants in the backseat. The hard-on I have is not much of anything. The man's pants are brown, light tan slacks, wet in spots. I put my hand on his knee. My friend has already marked the man. The man starts drooling into my ear. My

6

friend pulls back onto the Interstate. There's no way to stop, no-where. My hand holds a handful of the man, down where I am held by his hands. He is trying to make me harder. I go to hold him around the balls, like it's instinct, to join in. I think that I never want to do this again, not like this. I squeeze lightly.

I don't want him to think he bothers me, though, that I am affected by him. His hands are dry paper. I don't want my friend to hear me whisper, ask the man if he has anything, a condom.

His hair runs over my lips. Yes, yes.

He puts his mouth down on me again. I pull a hand of his thin hair up by its roots, jerk his head up, yanking before he can let another drop of his spit drool anywhere near. His hands are tiny, frightened little lizards. I don't want his mouth on me without anything protecting me, between us.

I don't want your mouth on me without a condom.

I'm so unexpectedly forceful he decides we best end the ride.

He leans over the seat and tells my friend to drive back to the park. Then he sits there beside me, apologizing over and over again, how he's sorry, he's so sorry.

Fuck you. We are still driving.

We sit in silence further away from each other in the backseat, the man and me.

Once we pull back into the park, up to my friend's parents' car, I let myself out, thinking the whole time that the man probably liked my friend better than me. Others circle us in the distant flickering halogens like blind moths.

7

It Takes Me Forever to Get Home

dorm

I could have lived with my first roommate who would turn the air-conditioning on so cold I could barely sleep without blankets and blankets laid upon me. It was warm where he was originally from, Florida. I went there once when I was young.

duplex

I could have stayed in half of a house for a home. I moved there from the dorm so lovers, older men almost always, wouldn't have to feel so uncomfortable coming up to my floor. Then there was also Philippe, a French boy.

My first winter there I couldn't sleep like a normal person. Not that I had ever slept that normally. I'd rely instead on a number of men to invite me over. I don't know what was wrong with me, why I couldn't just get a good job. I wanted to do other things with my life, though. I dreamed that I wasn't going to die working day after day so I could one day buy a TV, go to the movies, get a car, etc. I slept in front of the oven, instead. I closed off the kitchen with a thick black blanket hung in front of the doorless doorway, to try and keep in whatever warmth I could create most cheaply. All night coils burned orange.

All day I wrote in a diary.

One winter these two men I knew would let me come over and share their bed with them. It's nice for a while, but then it just gets too weird. I fall in love with one and not the other, and there's never going to be enough room for the three of us to live together, so I go.

But before, when it was just me and the one I had fallen in love with, the way I fit up against him in the small bed in the spare room, since he didn't think it was right to sleep with me without his boyfriend there, in the big bed the two of them and so often the three of us slept weekends in, his golden skin glided along me. I was under his arm like under a wing. He was much older than me, and I was romantic. They were Henry and June although they were both men. I was going to be a writer, and I had to live like a bohemian if I really wanted to make it, I thought. I was still just a kid, really.

I outgrew them. I started sleeping with one of their friends. He was rather rich, and he was an eccentric. He liked young things like me. The heaters in his house were like those old units I remembered from elementary school. Periodically, over that winter we were together, he had to check the boiler in the basement to make sure it was not overheating, not too low on water. I would be fine as long as he was there.

I spent the days at tables in the corners of coffee houses, in front of windows, writing entries in my diary about who may have loved me, who maybe still did, on some level, by the way he held me, who it would be best for me to believe I could live with, one day, have a life with.

divorce

Since we were two men sleeping together in trust for so long, he worried about me. He jokingly calls the decent place he helped me get for myself once he wanted me further away my settlement. At least the heat works, I thought to myself.

I donate old space-heaters to the Salvation Army. No one shares my body with me all winter. Near spring, there's one younger than they usually tend to be. He lectures me on how to make it warmer in my house. I say it's dangerous to keep the gas heaters running all day when I'm not there, like he'd like me to, so it will already be nice and warm at night when I bring him in, home. He says he can tell sex really means something more than sex to me, from sleeping with me.

On top of me, his skin is a pale light in the room. We're both winter white. His nose is Roman, brown eyes deep above his tender lips, more pink than red. We change places often in the bed. I lie over him like another cover. I don't want him to ever go. Blood runs inside, under his hands, thawing around and around. He tells me how good my skin feels to him.

I already know I'm going to move before another year, though, unless he does something to try and keep me here.

I watch the flames in the gas heater glow purple, orange, hot blue, flicking upward like tongues of feathers that coo. I fall asleep across from the dazzle of heat's display.

It's so cold with him here it's warm.

inside denial

It hurts him to look at me, because he's still got feelings he can't think about right now. He roams all over my face for somewhere to focus, since I won't meet his eyes. He doesn't want to look at me any lower. He could reach out and brush me there.

He notices that I'm sleeping in the hall now, that I've moved the mattress out there from the bedroom.

That way it's easier for me to feel more centered in my own house.

He wants to see how long it's going to take for me to look at him. That's all he's doing here.

He notices I've been trying to cut my own hair again, haven't I?

He can tell. I didn't have a mirror here when I tried to do it. I asked him if he'd help me fix it, the easiest thing I could do to try and change myself. I tell him I'm going to move to Europe. I just want to hear him try to talk me out of it. I follow him into the bathroom, hold my head over the sink for him. He takes the clippers back over my half-assed army cut.

He can only even it out by going all the way down to the scalp. I remind myself I'm not feeling anything. His touches aren't meant to provoke me. A brown shirt accentuates the sun on his skin and makes him look more bronze. Things keep changing color in front of me. We both know somebody who's in love now. He was one of our friends.

outside a diner

It hurts him to look at me, like it hurt me to see him the other night inside the diner, loud, at a window table, with a party of friends.

For a moment I forgot and thought he might still be who he once was, for me.

But no, he's with another boy.

I know him. He once posed nude for a friend of ours.

with details

What little light left in the day shines in front of me through his ear. He turns to face me as he takes my head in his hands. The blood inside his skin glows, lit from behind. We are still in my bathroom, together. The setting sun shines through the window and then through him.

He's washing up to go, now that he's finished.

It's easier to think of him as wounding me, to try and stay away from him in the future, to change my address eventually.

Then there will be no mistaking there is no way for him to find me, no way for me to extend myself any longer, once I become someone he has no prior claim to, someone else who no longer relates to what he once knew, before he moved on.

A Model Love

I answered an ad to shed my clothes. I'd done it once before, life modeling. No big deal. I needed the extra money, and I was awake enough to sit still. I called the man, and we set up a date.

He picked me up in his truck. It was a blue truck. He had to tell me what he would look like, too, so I'd know who he was.

He had this show opening up in New York soon, he said. It's a big world out there.

He paints on wood.

Away from the college campus, his studio is about a thirty minute drive.

How do you get a man to invite you into his space? What do you have to give him?

Once we get there, he warns me there are no facilities, so I might want to go outside before we get started, if I need to. It's February. I pee while he goes inside and prepares. I come in from the cold to join him. I move through sheets of plastic further into his studio, towards his voice. He tells me he once had a place set aside inside for changing, but not anymore.

Take off your hat.

Then I'm supposed to take off my clothes, while he finishes setting up, just another second and he'll be ready. I can put my clothes over there on the desk.

I'm a little nervous now about how I might come across to him, like he might think I just wanted to do this, that the fact I'm getting paid doesn't matter at all to me. If I don't give him what he wants I'm not going to be able to come back. And I'll like being inside here with him. It will give me somewhere to go during the day, to feel connected to something, a part of something happening.

He seems instantly pleased with my body.

Yeah, I'm going to work just fine. He says something like that. He likes me because I'm so flexible. You know, you've got a dancer's body.

Most men really aren't so limber. He walks around me.

His heart beats, like mine does.

I try to stay how he wants me now, there, try not to squirm on the used couch I'm placed on, get used to how he puts me. He adds a couple of cushions, removes some other ones from under my legs, knees, places another on top of the stack of pillows behind my head. It's nice to have someone touching me again, approving of the way I look. You're young, that's what my boyfriend before had said. You have your whole life in front of you, and one day we could maybe be together again. The painter's hands will soon be my cover. Every once in a while, he steps back and regards me, makes a frame in the air with his hands out in front of him, his eyes looking through his hand-frames at me.

He regards my body intensely, from other views, angles, sides.

He's looking at me in the way I want to be looked at. I'll have a boyfriend one day who will want a boyfriend who does things like modeling.

Even though the initial session actually takes up almost three, the painter only gives me two hours' wages. I don't say anything. He says after opening up his wallet, what he'd like to do is set up a second date.

He means to draw me, just get some preliminary sketches out of the way. Then he'll do the actual painting. We both bring out our calendars, to figure out next when we are both going to be free. He'd like to try to get me together in a group with some other guys, too, he says. If I'd be willing to do that.

That's what he's going for, he tells me, to show a more complete picture.

I planned on never returning again where I'd come from before. I can make in an hour just a little more than what I make working at the coffeehouse. All it involves is holding the pose. He arranges my body, sets me down on cushions on the couch, comes up closer to touch me up, again, puts me back closer to the place I've relaxed ever so slightly from, when I've shifted. Across the room from me, he draws. He tells me to look another way, faces my face another direction, talks to me about art this and art that, asks me if I've ever done this before.

Once, for a class. The class was on anatomy, drawing the form of the human body. The students were only supposed to be thinking about that, keeping their minds on their schoolwork. The professor teaching the class kept saying how good my muscles were. You could see them clearly, because I was so skinny then, not much besides the long muscles under my skin he was in the process of defining for them.

I only did it once, never could go back. The whole time I was lying there on my back on the small white wooden stage at the front of the class, in front of them, under one bright white light trained down on me, I was thinking of myself in pieces. The next day I called the school and told them I was sick, that I wasn't going to be able to make it in to model for the anatomy class.

I thought this time it could be different, since it was just him, one man. It seemed like an easy way to make money, even though I didn't really know him. We talked for a couple of minutes the first day in the coffeehouse before he brought me back to his studio out in the country. He offered to buy me a cup of coffee before we went, but I said I was fine. I wasn't all that attracted to him, not initially. What was it between two people? What drew one to another?

I guessed he was around thirty. He graduated from some master's program in fine art, told me the program, but soon I forgot the name.

He wears his hair in one long black braid. He bars the metal door with a beam of wood, once we're inside his studio, locks the outside. He tells me I'm good, that he wishes he could pay me more, that he likes what he's getting from me.

Most boys your age like to go to the bar.

He's never seen me in the bar, where everyone goes, where they all go to meet people.

I start stripping again, getting ready for him, shirt first. It's warmer in the studio today.

Here. Put it over here. He reaches out his hand for my shirt. The sooner I get into the pose he's got for me, the less I have to just stand there naked. That's how the sessions work. I stand there wondering if I should cross my arms in front of my chest, or cup them in front of me. I wait for him to tell me what to do next, tell me how he wants me. He tries to make small talk because he must be aware it's less uncomfortable when we do talk like I'm not standing there naked.

Your boyfriend before was the one who'd needed all the attention.

The painter says just because two men, or even more, are naked together, doesn't necessarily mean they're queer. This makes me imagine him with me on the couch, undressed, bending down there with me, sliding the white T-shirt he draws in up over his chest, just to prove his point.

The shirt would graze his Adam's apple, stretch up over his head, pull at the long braid at the back of his head, his arms raised over his head.

There had been nights before he'd left that I thought I knew where my boyfriend might be. Nobody ever knows where I am. One day I'll have to find someone else.

I meet the man painting me at the coffeehouse, and then we drive out.

Do you know any guys who might want to come out and pose with you? Our bodies would touch, if they ever did. He'll sketch how our bodies overlapped, with more men in the picture now, lying all there together on the couch.

One. I know one guy.

He's just some guy in town everybody knows and makes a big deal out of how he models on campus for all the art classes, how much he loves it. I only sort of know him. He's not really that attractive, to me, but touching him might still be erotic. I think the same of the painter, after just lying there under his eyes so often. My hand goes down to touch the couch as I ease myself into the new position he has for me. He says my eyes look different when I'm lying down, like a painting from the fifteenth or sixteenth century people go home and dream about.

We had a couch like this when I was a little boy. I used to watch my father fall asleep on it in his white T-shirt. Once, the cigarette in his hand fell down onto the brown floral pattern of forest, burning a small black hole through, before his cigarette went out. I imagine the hole is there now, on his different couch, fingering the brocade my body will eventually wear down. The painter is acting like all the other men I've been with, how they seem surprised the first time they undress me. Only he's not helping at all, just waiting, watching while I do it to myself, waiting for us to get started.

How come you never wear underwear?

It's just too much clothes.

Down my chest a little, down under my left nipple, towards the side, I wonder if the painter notices, sketches my mole. My button, that's what my boyfriend before had called it, as he pushed against it. I show next to no emotion on the couch, staying how he wants me to stay. Right now the painter is viewing me as, simply, a body. I try not to seem too eager to converse, too interested in his opinion of me. He's painting me like he would paint anyone who happened to land here on his couch. I haven't endeared him to me with any of my little characteristics yet. I do what he wants me to do, being only a boy's body.

Still, his hand feels different on me, my body, feels different to me now, different than the first day when we just shook over introductions.

Can you call me during the week? So we can set up another date? He wants to do a couple more sketches before he starts the actual painting.

I become more and more comfortable returning to him, as he's no longer such a stranger. It starts to seem natural to strip for him. He makes me more and more at ease on the couch, that barrier that gives us each our own place. Everyone he starts working on, eventually finishes, kneels or drapes or lies here on this couch, dirty with us.

Does he know what it feels like to want this? Maybe I step out of my clothes this time a little too quickly. It could be almost like I'm daring him to touch me. I cross my arms in front of my chest, as he takes my elbow, puts his big hand on my back, and leads me over to the couch, puts me down on it again.

This is the moment at which he might kiss you.

There I go. My Adam's apple bobs. I've done this all before, with other men, folded my arms like I just did. My boyfriend before pointed out how he thought my folded arms were cute, how I did that whenever I undressed for him, waited there beside his bed for further, more directions. This is all only in my head. I try to remind myself being naked is only being naked.

It's so quiet in the room, just the scratch of his charcoal stick. My body occasionally feeling the accidental scratch from the broad band of one of his fingernails, the callus on his thumb.

Look what he's done, made this slight red spot on my skin, as he was rearranging me.

It will go away.

How am I feeling?

Fine.

Comfortable?

Yeah. I've been standing up all day. It feels good to be on the couch. It feels good against my skin.

He laughs, goes across the concrete, cluttered floor of the studio, turns on another one of the small electric heaters he points at me, to keep it from getting too cold for me. Is the temperature all right? The heater is only blowing the cold air in the room around.

Fine.

It's March. It's still cold in the stilted air in there. He's standing above me. I'm already down on the couch on my back, knowing the position by heart by now.

Though occasionally he will do something different with my hands.

He bends down closer over my head, face, mouth, to rearrange the pillows under me. It's quiet except for the umm of the heat that blows out and around. I try to think of myself as something else, a fish, because the closeness of his body is then suddenly too near. It surprises me, and I jump lower, my thoughts not so appropriate.

You're in love with someone, aren't you. Who?

The first time I felt myself thinking like this, I ran through all the other things in my mind I could possibly be than this boy in this body, and I came up with the thought of myself all in ice, a cold body of water, fixated on that. I thought of breaking the surface, the cool, open air. It didn't matter how deep down or without light, far down from everything I was, my body would still be able to breathe.

I finger with my hand draped behind me, out of his line of vision, the feel of the couch. It feels like the brocade pattern could be little opened roses, raised up slightly. I smooth the fabric all over with the brush of my body. I try not to notice too much here. My stomach knots the longer I hold the pose, my knees bent up together, pulled close up to my chest. I'm almost this U on its side.

My weight is suspended by the edge of the couch from falling towards the floor.

It's what he wants, stillness that can read as movement.

My empty stomach mumbles lightly again. Just a little longer. He rinses a brush. The black tip dips down into a clear glass of water in his hands now gray.

I made myself learn to take anything with my boyfriend before. I didn't want to disappoint him, ever. I wasn't going to move a muscle if he wanted me to be so still.

I blink open my eyes, blue.

He's sketching my left leg now. If I fall asleep here, I could shift slightly.

It's OK if you want to close your eyes. I wonder if he only remembers the color. My hair is blonde. My build is still what is commonly called a swimmer's.

His charcoal pencil floats me there down on the wood board.

Round and round his hand goes, up and down, and there I am in an hour or two, some trace, version of me.

He picks up a piece of a mirror from a corner of the studio, looks into it with his back to the sketch he's been working on, to see how it's progressing, how it's heading. Black charcoal lines chalk a thick outline over white paintbrush strokes. There's the occasional stray line, too, to show motion outside of me, myself, what moves around me.

Can I hold the pose for a little longer?

He's concentrating, so I stay quiet. I have potentially as many wounds as there are openings.

I fold my clothes in a pile on the desk in his studio, my hindquarters still sore from yesterday. It's not until it's time to let go of my body every day that I feel free, finally. The release from here becomes its own sort of daily orgasm. When the pose starts to hurt, I will start biting the insides of my cheeks. I know he can't tell what I'm doing. I work less and less skin down between the gnaw, increasing the pain elsewhere on my body to transfer the sensation to something more acute. If that doesn't work I move onto the little red tip of my tongue. I don't want him to think I need a break, any break. I close my eyes a little, flex, unflex myself almost imperceptibly, tightening to release. I know he won't be finished with me until he feels he's sufficiently captured the language of my body. I'll suddenly look like a different boy, marked down by his hand. It will no longer be just me, completely, as he paints me as some sort of fable, one fed grapes by someone else in a background.

Occasionally there's March sun through the skylight, as it passes over the studio's glass roof, or a cloud moves out of the way. Light filters through layer after layer of plastic he places over windows, to help keep the drafts out, his studio just an old gray shack.

Things dissolve then in the air in front of me as the sun goes down.

It gets harder and harder for him to see me, for me to see him. Out of the corner of my eye, my cheekbone is now drawn in shadows. My knees clack together. He tells me to stick out my chest a little more.

I press my back down against the couch. His boards, the wood he paints on, started out all white, prepared for the day's sketch. An expanse of black emerges like disturbed water, new lines of charcoal. He says let's call it a day.

Once, earlier, one of my boyfriends, one of the first I'd ever been with, picked me up when I put my arms up around his neck, cradled me underneath my legs held in his arms, carried me off in the house through to his bed. I was able to let myself go with him.

Later, there will be an attempt to pick me out from all the parts, the sketches left lying around everywhere. He wipes his hands on his pants, squatting down beside me on the couch, says just relax that one finger.

He moves my hand, back, forth, then back against my chest, spreads my fingers out, then balls them back more into a fist.

He says this about me. He says there, those are more interesting lines.

I touch my ring finger to my little toe, big toe, holding onto my feet, stretch.

Today I'm going to have my arms behind me, my legs curled up under me. He says he's really been thinking a lot about the pose, wants to try some other things eventually.

He gets a new stick of charcoal from the box, an action like lighting another cigarette for him.

I lie on the gold velvet couch and close my eyes. I hear him sketching, rubbing me again in the charcoal. I open my eyes to see he's wearing his white T-shirt again. I'm supposed to be turned up towards the ceiling, but he notices I've moved my head, comes over to reposition me.

Then his hand is on the side of my body, just resting there, lightly on the flank of me.

He's charcoal marking me now, my body. Look at my skin. He has a finger, a thumb, on either side of my face, moving me, my head, by my temples.

He touches my cheeks, his black fingertips up against my skin.

I bear his smudge-prints, and he pulls away. I'm sorry, he apologizes for the mess.

No problem. I look at the way my body's huddled, change how my face looks by grinning at him.

You can relax for a second, if you want.

Thanks, I say, going limp.

With his black sweatshirt he brushes off my face, says it looks like I've got dirt on me.

It's not. It's the traces of his charcoal.

I wish he would touch me with his spit, that he would wet my face that way, with something inside him, rub it in a little more, to ease this friction, to make it go away a little better.

You look like it's Ash Wednesday or something.

I know soon we will be done. He told me yesterday he has another boy who is going to start posing for him. But I don't know where he found him.

I'd like to get the two of you together, the painter says.

And I don't say anything.

He'd like me to hook, twine my body around, hold still with, this other boy for a couple of hours, the two of us naked. I'm trying not to talk to the painter too much because I don't want to get too close to him. The painter knows I like men. I told him that the first day we were driving out to his studio.

Some of them don't like it when you use the word boyfriend. I watch the buildings and parks pass us, up in the front of his truck, sitting beside him, not wanting to look at him too directly, in light of how we would be in his studio together.

Again, he feels the need to apologize for how little he's paying me. No problem. I lie. It's easy work, craving someone as likely to fall out of line as me.

I will learn to be more and more pliant.

It will become easier, the longer he draws me in. I'll fall asleep on his couch. I'll dream of his white sheets covering me. In less than a month, he'll have to be all finished with me, because then his show will be opening.

That's all for now, he'll wake me up by saying.

We drive back to town, and he starts trying to make conversation about how he thinks the world is falling apart. I don't want him to just drop me off at home. There's nothing there for me.

He points out the window. You see all these roadblocks, towers, all these bulldozers everywhere? All they're doing is just making it worse. It upsets him.

He says he's got to show me to some of his friends.

This one friend of his, this professor, he's doing another one of his art films. I know him, don't I?

I'd like him. He's always needing boys to get nude for these things. I should give him a call. He tells me I'm handsome enough. He tells me he'll put in a good word for me, if I want.

Anonymous Glory

There are certain men that can be located in movies or magazines, and then there are more you can find in stalls.

They meet at times I'm not aware of until later. Before class, first thing. Some afternoons, late evenings. But seldom as late as I'm out.

They've all got someone or somewhere to get back to, a wife or dorm.

I keep walking into the men's room at the Student Center all the time because once I want to walk in and see, know, there were already two guys with their bodies together in there, and I could see, watch. I could know, feel, rest assured.

It's not only me, I reason, at least a handful of them must be like me.

You never know what the men will look like. They just list their dates. You can see a little through the sliver of the closed stall doors, where it doesn't quite meet, though.

I sit on a couch in the Student Center, on the lower level. Someone will walk outside, turn back to look at me. I know they've seen me. They go to the parking lot and then walk back in, follow me up the stairs. They watch me buy a ticket to the movie playing in the theater on the upper level.

I want to come in contact with something other than an image on a screen.

I feel too self-conscious, and this is one way to lose myself.

If one of those boys, men, follows me into the dark, I will ask him what he wants. I might ask him to follow me next from upstairs down to the lower level men's room.

I unzip in front of the toilet, getting hard. I move into one of the stalls rather than just standing there in front of a urinal.

You can hear others releasing themselves in there, can hear even though you can't see, yet, their zipper noises. It heightens your senses.

I make rustling sounds, pulling off pieces of tissue paper, letting everyone know I'm there, in one of those stalls, in case someone hasn't already looked down for my pair of shoes.

I like to hear their breathing, words to themselves, the way they would talk if I were closer, closer to them, skin sliding against a palm. Holding myself, thinking about it, I keep coming back.

I have to have a destination.

I keep coming back to the Student Center.

The movie is already started, although I didn't really want to see it anyway. I want to see what men who like men like me look like.

Not the flickering reel.

There, inside the stall on the lower level, I could be anyone.

He comes in right after me, into the stall next to mine. Immediately. In after me, like he was following, trailing me. That feeling you get when you're walking down the street sometimes. It creeps into my jeans.

I was just about to unzip anyway.

He might look like a football player. A lot of the students here do. Those are the kind of boys who come to the Student Center. His shoes are Nike. He taps his foot up and down a couple of times, and I watch the swish of the check bob, the one I can see, near me, by the extra room at the bottom.

He is sitting down next to me.

He is only down for a second, though, before he gets up, fastens his pants up, zips, and goes out of the stall.

I don't do anything. I just stand there in the stall that was next to his, alone now, facing the head of the toilet like I'm about to piss, but I'm getting too hard to do anything else. Earlier, we could both have been thinking of the same thing.

Often when I come here, there are bodies all around me on movie nights.

In a second, quickly, the stall door on my other side is swung. It's the same shoe as before. He sits down again and taps his shoe up and down, so I tap mine back.

Morse code to show we're not alone.

I want him to start jerking off, whispering low to himself, just loud enough for me to overhear.

I remember the time I went into the men's at the library. Some man, I could see he was wearing boots, was breathing to anyone, everyone, yeah. Show me that dick.

Someone was there. I was. I could hear him.

Some time after that, there was another behind a closed stall door, another, muttering he just wanted to suck, get sucked, just wanted to.

The air is heavy basement, stale. Big machines click on and off, humming. The heat in pipes rattles. My legs standing there locked get weak.

Everyone wants a mouth on them here, rather than a holding hand.

I'm still standing up, with myself in my hands. I want to test the limits of constraints.

The Nike is angled more and more towards me until it is under the partition of stall, sliding up next to me and my leg, foot. I'm weak in my knees when we touch shoes.

Then, it looks like the guy is getting up again. The latch on the stall with the Nikes to my left doesn't click open, though.

Someone else has come in.

He's standing up in there now. I look down at his shoe at an even more protruding angle. He's trying to tell me quietly not to go.

I bend down and can see his inner thigh skin, his jeans pulled down low to his ankles, his naked leg, his belt tapping against the tile, sliding gently up and down over it.

I could touch him if I lowered myself a little more.

He has on a gold watch.

The light purple head of his erection is being pulled on by

him. He's doing it for me. He has small, delicate fingers I notice. He lets me see his eye next. I could just touch him.

Once the guy not part of what's really happening here leaves, the Nikes come out of the stall, stand there before mine still closed. I wonder do I open the door to him, do I let him come in?

I want to jerk-off in proximity, take comfort in the fact that he's doing it, too. We are all doing it. The bathroom is quiet. I don't know what I'm supposed to do, what he expects me to do. I don't know.

There's a slice of him that's appealing. It's his shrewd eye, lips cruel and thick, this pout of undisguised lust for me, this. I can see he's biting his own lips. We are just trying to take care of some basic need.

Then, he is forced back into the stall beside me because another guy comes into the men's room. I see again the naked inner thigh, jeans down around his ankles. He is beside me in another stall. He is kneeling down on the tile. He is craning down below, trying to angle up under the small space, meant to keep us separated, fit himself up under there.

I go ahead and let him see me pulling on myself a little. Yes, I'm like him.

As soon as the other guy in here with us leaves, he can go ahead and make a definitive move. I wonder how to get out of this now.

Back into my jeans I stuff myself, that little action almost making me come, but I am able to control myself.

He is right behind me leaving the men's room, following me.

I head for the water fountain, trying to recover there drinking gulps of water, stopping, wondering why he won't just leave. It's over. I've ended it.

He goes to gather together a book he left open earlier and out, a spiral pad on top, on one of the student couches. With his class notes, studying in a position he could watch the men's room door from, he was keeping track of who was going in and coming out. He must try everybody.

I'm taking the stairs to get out of the building two at a time, but know he's still following me. I'm trying to walk the wet campus fast enough to discourage him behind me.

Halfway up a hill, I can tell by the shadows he is right behind, close, following, still. His shadow is approaching mine, coming up to it, almost right up on top of me. What could he possibly say? He saw I wanted something bad enough to want anything. Why wouldn't I want him? He's still behind me.

He had to have seen me jerking off. We were practically doing it together.

When he has finally almost caught up with me, his voice isn't much louder than a whisper, with tones of a concurrent groveling, not too unpleasant, though slightly sticky. Hey man.

But I don't stop walking.

Hey man. He's finally caught up with me. His voice is this shadow at my side. Do you wanna go jerk-off somewhere?

I recover lamely, say, I only do that for money.

I've been thinking of the movie playing upstairs all night.

You only jerk-off for money?

Yeah. Sorry.

But by now he has already turned around, like disappointment is just another emotion to be accepted. He doesn't follow any further. Every couple of blocks, I turn and check to make sure, hoping even a little he might have changed his mind.

Town

Isn't it a whole new town now that we aren't together? He says that like it's good.

It's a town where everyone gets drunk but me. A town where I no longer have anything to do. I am no longer in school here.

It's a town where I know how to find him. At any given moment in the day, it wouldn't be that hard. There's really no reason for me to go looking for him, though.

I know exactly how far I can go here.

I stopped half-way.

I could have worked towards having my own house here one day. I could have had a place, friends, my own mailbox, a better job. I could work in a coffeehouse for the rest of my life, if all else fails.

I have this unreasonable want to cut myself off from everyone I once knew, anyone that saw I was once his, something else. I stand at the window in the house and look out at the street, the cars gliding up and down, how dark it gets every single night. The only future I know is the swallowing of myself, the going from day to day, from place to place, going from where I work to where I stop when it's over.

Undated Days

blank book

He made this book in art class, a course on papermaking and book-binding. He learned to press things into the pulp. Some girls he knew put in petals of rose. He wanted his project to be more personal, so he ended up shaving off a little of his chest and pubic hair, added that to his mixture.

The book was the only thing he could think to give me as a going away present, back when we both thought I was going to travel, to get away from just hanging around town, now that I'd graduated. He thought the book would really mean something to me, the only thing that would mean enough. I was leaving the next morning.

He showed up to give it to me, my only Christmas present so far, to take with me. Christmas wasn't that far away. He wanted me to wait to open the present, even though I could tell it was a photograph.

Everything was packed up in my room. I told him he could have my bed, the good mattress. I thought he might start touching me again, when he asked me if I felt safe about leaving. He warned me he couldn't stay all night.

I'm leaving early in the morning, anyway, I said.

We went to bed together.

When traveling didn't feel right, I thought foolishly it might help me to go back to my mom's house and rest there a while. She said I needed to get myself back. I needed to get away from all the same faces in the town, the fact that everyone knew this photographer had stopped what we were doing. Once at my mom's, I placed the blank book he gave me under my pillow, that way during the night part of me could still grope something that had to do with him. There didn't seem to be any other options left in town. I was so used to moving my hand back and forth along the feel of the book's cover, the slight raise of his hair in the dark that recalled height, size, taller than me, bigger, the way he locked his legs around me, and underneath me he unbuckled.

I'd written down dreams of him like this, prone, in the past.

On Christmas Eve, I unwrapped the photograph. I remembered how he had said I was special when he gave it to me, even though he wasn't showing that anymore with his body. I had been hoping something would be revealed when I unwrapped the photograph, that there would be something he thought, felt, couldn't quite put into words, staring up at me. It was a picture of a Christmas tree, and a bike halfway in the frame.

Typical, something he could have given to anyone.

36

family, friends

I've gone back to the town and am helping a family move from one house they were renting to one they've just bought. They're friends. The expecting mother asks me if I'm seeing anyone these days. I can't remember if I ever told her about him. She wouldn't know from the bars what he's up to. She has little time left for those low lights of whatever bar everyone is going to that week, now that she has one child and another on the way.

Then she does say his name, says what about him, do I ever see him out lately? She wonders what he's been up to, just making conversation, but I think she must know.

I tell her I hear he's going to India, although he has been saying that forever. That's how I answer from now on anybody who happens to ask me about him, India, as I try to tell myself he was nothing if not predictable, someone who once gave me a picture of myself I kind of liked.

Someone makes a bet out at the bar one night, one thousand dollars, that when he settles down eventually, it'll be with a man. Right now he needs to figure things out, focus on the direction of his life. That's what he told me.

Everybody thinks it's funny, except one of his ex-girlfriends and me. They were together for a number of years. It was the last substantial relationship he had before coming to live in the town. She eventually followed him down, goes out drinking now where he does. In some ways, to me, they still seem together.

I keep trying to defend him to all of my friends. I think partly because I tried so hard to know who he really was. I can't seem to admit I might have made a mistake with him. I must know why he's acting the way he is, because he needs to figure out who he really is. That's all. I want to believe I did know him, really saw him, when he was reaching down to guide me inside him. Having once been there with him like that, I feel sorry for him now.

In many ways, I am like his ex-girlfriends.

first date

That night I had nothing better to do so I went by the bar where he checks IDs at the door, saw him stacking chairs upside-down on long wood tables. That's how late it was when I was wandering around. He saw me outside the glass front windows, waved and walked closer, inside towards me, turned a key in a lock and let me in to say he'd found twenty dollars that night on the floor, wanted to know if I'd like to go get something to eat with him later than late.

There was that twenty-four-hour restaurant that would still be open.

Sure. I said I'd wait for him.

He still had some sweeping to do, but he'd meet me there. He had nothing better to do either, once he got out of there.

I bumped his knee on purpose under the table. He asked me if I wanted to go.

By then the streets were almost completely empty, one or two cats and us. I said I'd walk him to his bike. No one could see us, so he asked me if I wanted to hang-out. It was a little past three in the morning by the clock on the bank. All the bars had closed at two.

I asked his house or mine.

Mine, so we wouldn't have to worry about being too loud. He rents a room in a large house from one of his photography professors. We went back to my place. That became all this.

girls

He was just experimenting, the ex-girlfriend tells everyone. She doesn't want me to get any ideas.

I want to remind her he's a photographer and not a scientist.

She tells everybody in the bar one night that it was just a phase. He was going through a phase. She's afraid the past will cease, no longer mean the same thing for the two of them. But he's not seeing me anymore.

I try not to dwell too much on the way I eased into him, how easy it was with him. I try not to notice when we're in the same restaurant and he's out with another girl, a different one, one he told me he once thought he was in love with, so in love. The two of them are having lunch, so he looks deep into her eyes. I have to make myself get up. I'm walking out of there. I'll see him around.

on the street

For a moment, I thought he might always want me there, between his legs, the way he reached back and wrapped his free hand around the iron of the frame of his bed.

On the wall behind his head was a poster from that movie we all wanted to be in for some reason, two men acting like hustlers frozen on motorcycle back. The one behind is holding onto the leather of the other's jacket, the coat gripped into his fist. He stopped for a moment that night to ask me if I had anything, before we continued, and I thought he meant protection, so I got up to go get a condom from the bathroom. He only meant lubrication, though, and he looked slightly insulted, pulling the white rubber I'd put on off me when I got back to the bed from the bathroom.

I was just leaving the house. He comes this way to go home sometimes when he's not driving his car or riding his bike. It's such a small town. It's a nice walk for him.

He walks down my street another day. He doesn't live very far away.

He is under a navy hood, looks shady and good, serious, god. Like some attraction, some attachment, like he means anything to me. I try to pretend not to see him. This only helps the situation slightly. I'd been hoping desire would thin the less it was fed, presumed he was seeing someone else, somewhere else. He must have been. I set a goal for myself, decide if he hasn't made any definite move back towards me by the time I fill up the blank book he gave me, it's all going to be over.

the chorus

At concerts now we pretend not to see each other, don't stand too close, not even for the sake of trying to appear normal. I have a feeling we both know it would be too tempting, that late at night, and we just can't anymore, for some reason he's decided.

We aren't still. Other bodies surge around us in certainty. We are what's left of some couple of nights. He'll take somebody else back to see what's left of his studio, where it used to be so much better, in the back of the coffeehouse where I work, that big building divided into spaces.

He drives down the street later in his white car.

He doesn't have to work tomorrow morning. It's his day to sleep in. His car won't be parked there in the lot I walk by so many times over the course of a day.

It's easier if we don't talk. He wants to be a strong person, he says.

When I see he's wearing those glasses that make him look smart, though, then I want to start seeing him all over again.

studio

I see him loading up his car with all the things from his studio. The men who've bought the building the coffeehouse I work in is in and his space is in the back of are going to knock down the wall he's set up a dark room behind, make the whole thing one big place, expand it all.

He's got to clear out soon. They have plans of turning the coffeehouse into another bar, eventually. Pool tables will take up the space where he once developed photographs, made phone calls, took me and more pictures, and I made coffee every morning at work.

He has a couple of weeks before all of his equipment must be moved somewhere. I watch him from across the street load up his car for the first of many trips, his loose pants riding down. That makes me remember his belt, the grain, the width, the square clasp of brass thin buckle, how he cut the rest of the belt's length off he didn't need.

Although it looked like something I wanted, it never developed further than taking off our clothes, going to bed together for a month or two, back to his studio those nights we didn't go to my place. He bends over to put another box in his car, and the belt isn't enough to keep his pants from slipping down a little more. I can't not look. From the other side of the road, I can't quite make out what's in the box. Soon his home away from home will be gone. I know that. He accepts the change like a mature person, holds his head resolved, keeps at his packing. He was leaving this summer anyway.

It becomes one more reason for him to look forward to that trip to India he's been planning all along.

the coffeehouse

I was reading a page in a book about becoming serious in life when he showed up behind me.

I could feel him, as I sat on a curb propped against a parking meter outside the coffeehouse. There's not much traffic today.

All the students are away on some break.

He hasn't shaved in awhile. He looks relaxed, partly glad to see me. He has his camera with him, and he is trying to look busy, like there's no way he can talk too long, got to get back to the errand of his walk. He doesn't want me to get the wrong impression, but he wants to know how my life's going. Anything specific?

Maybe he's not just being polite, making conversation.

Maybe he's alluding in some way he's anxious to have me back to see how well he's packed, how severely the plug has been pulled on the dark room. I think he's got to be able to tell I think of him every night, notice if he drives by my house as I happen to be looking out the window. It's still so easy for me to think of him sprawled on his back on that couch in the studio he's got for a few more days now. That's what I think about at night. I wonder if he's photographing girls or boys or both.

The next day I want to be weak and call him. Instead I walk downtown. His car is nowhere. I sit outside the coffeehouse and try to imagine myself somewhere else, pick a place, say England. It would be tea time there, no doubt, and I'd be far away from those corner tables with their wooden tops. I was often tempted to carve some sign of how we were once there.

A dog runs around in the afternoon light. I'm still on a bench with an open, romantic book in my hand. Kids in strollers are pushed by. I'm in the middle of trying to read a love story undisturbed. I fall back on the idea of his car as a white coach, things like that, as he pulls up, stops to talk to some girl at one of the outside tables, across from me, before he goes into the coffeehouse to begin his day.

He doesn't look over because he thinks maybe I'm trying to avoid him, the way I've got my face in the book, trying to forget about that day I noticed he didn't really come into where I work anymore, not when he knows, can see I'm around there. That was another day I saw him outside. It was easy to catch him through the windows that opened the front of the coffeehouse up to the streets. He placed his hands on a girl. They went to her shoulders, and then moved softly, as if he were trying to calm her.

For someone like her, he could do this. He would let himself make this gesture for her. I wanted to know what made me so different.

He was really drunk last night, I hear from everyone who wants to say his name in my face. I don't say I thought he wasn't drinking anymore. It's not my job to keep tabs on him. I know it's easier to pass the time drunk here. I know he's just biding his time until that day he goes to India.

He's gone back out to the bar for now with those guys who take pictures of drainpipes in attempts to document urban decay in our beautiful town.

Not wanting to hide what he was doing with me, that lasted about a week. He hasn't really given up anything but me. He talks about art, because how else will anyone take him seriously? Here, they still don't.

He'll get laid tonight if he gets the right girl drunk enough. That's all that matters. I imagine it takes place on top of all his packing boxes. His friends all watch him leave with her. One day he's celibate. We can't see each other anymore. The next night he's at the bar. He leers drunkenly at a German girl who all the guys I work at the coffeehouse with talk about, how that German girl looks just like a supermodel.

If he asked me what I was doing in the bar, I wouldn't say anything. Night after night, it's just second nature now, looking for someone like him.

We could have been really entering each other, not just each other's bodies.

Last night I watched him watch the door at the bar.

He sat in a brown chair propping open the door, glass. He's working for rent, food, film, and that trip to India eventually, another novelty, another shutter speed. I've shown him boys can be as difficult as all those girls he at one time or another once thought he was in love with.

He puts every little thing he can aside, clears his mind.

I often stand over off to the side of where all the boys who are his friends, who would never be caught dead doing with me what he's done, wait for him to finish his shift.

There's warmth from the proximity of so many bodies.

I no longer think I know what he meant when he said I had something no one else had. We're all here, and he's a good talker. It's what people in this town do, wait for something to happen. There will be another boy like me one day.

I hear the bartender brag about that one time he took me out to the woods.

Go to India, I just want to walk over to him and say.

He's waiting for this summer to go. It's even more boring here then. All the students who worship the artists for all their connections leave.

In India, he will do whatever he wants. No one will ever know. His bed voice is there somewhere behind me, in the hole of my heart, in a bar. I can overhear it. My pulse races over the page while I turn around. He is sitting at one of the window tables, watching the pedestrians all pass. He has joined another her, brushing her long hair out of her brown eyes.

I finger the small book I place in my pocket. His hairs are part of the material all sweaty with me.

No way I could confront him with this, all of this, as the bar fills up more. No way. I never did try to be romantic with him, at least not to his face. The place for anything is running out. It seems so obvious to me I've got all these feelings, and that I've got nothing left to do with them.

Now I Can't Kiss Anyone for a While

I work as much as possible. Six or seven days a week in a coffeehouse in a college town.

I've stopped living in the present, only dreaming of the future when I will leave all of this, even this country if possible.

I'm not making as much money as I used to, since the new owners have raised the prices. Counter tips have taken a turn for the worse, subsequently. Now I actually have to smile at all the customers if I expect them to dig down in their pockets for that extra quarter, since everything's been rounded up to an even number these days, and there's naturally no change left over for me.

I didn't raise the prices.

Every day I see the same customers, morning, noon, and night. Some, those who want to bother, keep up with a small card I'm supposed to track all their purchases on, so when they've bought enough they can get a free coffee. Part of my job is punching these heart-shaped holes into the cards. Get ten hearts, and you've got it made, any free drink you want, except for the juices.

One day I'm so bored, I'm slumped over the counter so I don't even have to prop myself up. I'm thinking thoughts meant to console like, at least I'm getting paid to just stand here. I hold the heart hole-punch in one of my hands, waiting for the next customer. I place the heart hole-punch around my lower lip, just fit it there, and am surprised that I can get it around.

I squeeze lightly, just to see what will happen, just enough to break the skin.

Pyrite

At the lake, the men have this tradition of night fishing. At this time, what they want to catch is more trustful.

It's at this lake that I first think I've found gold. I was going to be a true Balboa here. My stepfather soon strips my hopes. It's fool's gold. It's called pyrite. It floated in the water like flashes of light that swam under my hands, but was nothing permanent.

I pulled up handfuls of it and sifted it through my fingers, like I could become rich enough to do anything if I wanted if I could just hold on.

It settled.

Here, at this lake, I learned what a mud dauber's nest was, how the dried clay home was safe, abandoned once the wasp-like creature had laid her eggs. They hatched, and flew out.

You could keep these homes, pocket them, miniature souvenirs, reminders of your time at the lake.

A little further out in the body of water they sunk Christmas trees, to land on the bottoms where they'd become good homes for emerging schools of fish. Then, later, the men knew where they lived now and could be found. They'd marked the spots, went back late at night and sunk their lines, waiting for the lure of their bait to be taken, dipped under. They were yanked up as the unsuspecting fish tried to swallow hooks puncturing thin, translucent skin around their mouths. Entire beings were brought up out of their resting place in water, their natural habitat, just like that.

(out takes)

Initial Proposition

You were looking for a writer. Those were your words, not mine. You were singing to yourself, close to my ear. You were close enough for me to hear you were stumbling through the song you hadn't heard enough at the time, apparently, one that talked both about not enough time and wanting to be inside of someone.

I knew the feeling, and I liked the song. I said I liked it a lot. We moved on.

You call across the table we are sitting at to ask someone else if he knew another song. He didn't.

You said there was this line in that one that said something about a boy tasting wild cherries.

You had always wished it said the boy tastes like wild cherries.

Then, I thought you were trying to turn me on. It occurs to me.

I grabbed at the lapel of your jacket and felt something inside, pulling you down to my mouth. I said into your ear how I was going to bring you what you wanted. I was going to give you some writing.

You said dialogue was important. I was sweating.

It was summer. You could feel the wet on my skin with your hand on the back of my neck. I was just so hot.

I'm sorry. I'm sweating. I apologized.

It happens.

You looked into me with blue eyes recording, took my head, pushed it down, put it there against your stomach, overwhelming me.

The matches you had were from Europe. You wanted me to read the writing on the box to you. You knew I was taking a Romance language in school. It was a requirement.

Italian, I said.

Gruppo Saffa.

I said it how I thought it might sound. I wasn't very good in the class. I told you I didn't know what it might mean.

You repeated after me, and then you offered me a ride. You were giving me a ride home. The sky was incredible. Neither one of us could get over the sky that night.

As we neared my house, there was a white line in the middle of all the black, something cutting across the void of it.

As your car rolled up the hill to my house, there was something breaking on the horizon. You knew what I wrote.

Trick

This story here starts back when we'd only been sleeping together for six or seven months. Since this was the first time it had ever happened, I felt a little weird about it, his footing the bill for a plane ticket and a week or so in California where he was doing something work related. He thought I should go first class. I'd told him I'd never flown before.

This was back when I still sat around with my school books in the coffeehouse drawing ridiculous stickmen I pretended were representations of people just because I put this or that name underneath them, identifying who it was suddenly supposed to be.

The night before I was leaving for Los Angeles, he called to ask me what I wanted to do while there.

Have sex, I said. It was supposed to be kind of a joke.

What else?

I don't know. I don't care. I haven't really thought much about it. I just want to see you. Going to tar pits, seeing where some prehistorical animals were trapped, got stuck, sank, sounds OK to me. If that's what he wants to do, thinks I'd like.

He told me, before he hung up, that I was really going to like it there in California.

At the airport, none of the businessmen I am surrounded by on the flight pay much attention to us when he meets me at the gate, halfheartedly slips his arm around my shoulder, helps me with my baggage. I am wearing the black rubber coat he left with me the last time he was near.

I can stay here as long as he wants me to stay.

Back in the town where I go to school, he has a nice house that he only lives in half of the time. He spends almost as much time away, in hotels like the Chateau Marmont we check into after the airport, where we are given a bottle of wine and a basket of fruit. He thinks it's a nice gesture. I can't believe I'm actually here with him. No man's ever brought me to him like this before.

He wants to take a quick shower before we go out to dinner. I guess I could just go in and join him, but I'm still trying to get my bearings.

He comes out of the shower, naked, wants to know what I'm doing. I'm lying on the bed on my stomach, drawing in a notebook. He looks and says look, it's a firefly.

No, it's a flower. They are the only other things I can draw besides stickmen. I should know.

He lies down on top of my back. It feels good and warm, right.

He tells me I look like Brad Pitt.

Shut-up. I don't think Brad Pitt is sexy, only his broken tooth.

It's a compliment. Then he starts talking about some guy a little older than me who just wrote a really amazing screenplay.

I just wanted to stay in the room with him in the hotel.

He is putting on a suit, for dinner. I don't have any nice clothes The dirty duffel bag I hide on the floor of the closet has inside another pair of jeans I always wear, an orange T-shirt, a blue T-shirt, a change of socks, and no underwear. I don't know how long I'm staying.

As we are peeling out of the hotel's garage in a rental car, there's Keanu Reeves pulling in to park his motorcycle, just like *My Own Private Idaho*.

We go to eat in a fancy restaurant.

The apple pie served in the skillet it was fried in burns me, bad, on the underside of my arm near my elbow.

He asks me if I'm happy here?

I don't know.

Aren't you glad to see me?

Yes. Of course.

You know, it's OK for you to like it here.

After dinner, we go out to a bar, meet up with twin brothers there with a girl and another everyone is being mean to for some reason I don't catch.

So, one of the twin brothers says to me, trying to include me in the movie conversation, What do you do?

I feel his hand on my knee under the table, as he says, He's an artist.

The twin asks, Really? What medium?

Back in our room, I try to forget about how out of place I am feeling. Forget the way before dinner we stopped by a jean store where there was a photo exhibit, some sort of fund-raiser, and the woman at the door wanted to take a picture of me and him as we came in. They won't use that one.

He's a mostly settled man, successful at what he does, and I've just started college. I have my whole life ahead of me still. I go to unbuckle his belt with my teeth, but then the phone rings. It's a friend who always knows where he is.

I stare across the room at how he cradles it. I watch his face while he talks, his dark eyelashes, the chin stubble, his bright blue eyes, that flat freckle-like mole on his temple he's surprised I'm just now noticing.

That's there to lure you to me, he says once he hangs up the phone and I go to touch the place. Years later, he'll blush when the shape will change somewhat, and I point it out to him. It has changed.

Who can say if it's because I'm actually touching him again, there on that spot on his temple, that he colors, if he goes red out of fear that I am exposing some weakness he can't change about himself, pointing out how easily he could be hurt, seeing he's just as vulnerable as me? Maybe he just remembers this night.

Years later, who can say?

We are no longer that open with each other. We will just touch around the subject of that night.

I stand there touching nothing else but that place on his right temple.

Don't you want to finish the trick? He means my bit with the belt.

58

OK. I kneel down to the floor in front of him on the bed, do it.

It's easy enough.

That's some trick, he says. Then he jokes how he's impressed, look, he's applauding me. He means the way his dick pulses, up and down. I guess couples are supposed to be like that in bed, after a while, make jokes and stuff.

I place my hands flat against the floor, look down at my hands. How long since we've seen each other? Nothing's changed. Nothing at all.

He tells me to take off my clothes.

I take off my shirt. Take off your pants now.

You first.

I like the way he feels in my mouth, the heat of his skin against my lips. It's the first time we've done this without a rubber. He tells me he's going to come if I don't stop now. Once he confided in me that he didn't think monogamy was healthy, but he's been true to me, always, even though it's been hard, because we've both been waiting for this night for six months, since he convinced me to go test myself for him, so we could just do it and not worry anymore. If we were both clean, we had nothing to worry about.

Now here's where the confusion starts.

Hey, boy, wanna fuck?

I want to attribute my reluctance to the fact that he says wait here. He'll be right back. He wants to go put a rubber on. What did I think it would mean for nothing to be between us, to have him completely inside my skin? It has never felt safe.

Over dinner he talked about going out, buying a motorcycle.

He tried to enter me a number of ways, both of us kneeling on the bed, then behind me, then facing me, then on his lap. He seemed suddenly impossible, too much for me to take.

I remember my first boyfriend told me if you don't relax it just hurts.

I said his name.

I can't say anymore, just shut up and quit talking when he starts trying to swallow my earlobe.

I don't want there to be anything between us, I say.

He thinks he should wear a rubber.

He rolls off of me, doesn't say anything. It's not going to happen. He has a big day tomorrow. He gets up and goes into the bathroom, leaving me in the bedroom. He doesn't come back. It's so dark I can hear him rolling the rubber off, the way it's pulled away from sucking his skin snugly, then a cough. I hear him peeing, starting the water running for a shower.

The water hits the tiles.

I can't let myself stay here in this bed. He's paying for everything. He's paying for me, but it's not just the money.

I track through the hall loudly past the bathroom. I don't know ever if he heard me say that night under my breath how I hated him.

Our room had a balcony that overlooked the basin of the California valley. I went out there naked still, thought about earthquakes, the things you do in California. He came out wrapped in a white robe, sat down beside me. I'd moved back towards the door, against the wall, on the floor.

60

I wanted to try to give him a sense of what it was like inside me all that time, but his friends called to tell him they wanted to blow their heads off. If it kills you, then you know how it feels. We didn't really talk about things like that when we were together, like how he felt about me. It was one of these friends who once warned me to never fall in love with someone, never totally. He must have thought I'd take it lightly.

To turn to something, I touch his chest. His robe falls open, and I can see now he's even harder than earlier before in bed, now that he's here holding me, out on the balcony, and I'm crying for some reason.

I want to go home.

He shushes me, he knows, he knows.

But when I try to kiss him, he has to turn his face away.

The only place is the bed.

Since we're there, I want to do what I think I'm supposed to be doing. He follows me back saying we have to talk now. I don't have to let him fuck me.

I want you to fuck me.

Well, I can't do it now. There's no way I can do it now.

He laughs.

I think you can.

No, I can't.

He laughs again.

I'm not asking you to do it now, not right now.

He gets beside me in the bed. We'll just laugh all of this off.

In bed at his house, he once took my hand, put it on his

dick, asked me if I thought I was going to be able to take it, when the time came. He said he thought I could, and then he started counting down the months, long enough after me having been with nobody for him to be sure.

The first time I ever met him I grabbed onto his hand so tightly he said he was afraid I was going to break it.

You're overreacting. I don't know what's wrong with you. Why are you crying now?

Because I won't have unsafe sex with you?

I want to grab my clothes, my shoes, my socks. I'm going.

I'm getting out of here.

He wrestles me back down to the hotel bed, away from going to get my bag on the floor of the closet. I'm supposed to know he hates confrontations of any kind, any arguing.

I let him pin me to the bed, but once he expects me to just stay there, I try to shrug him off.

Stop patronizing me.

Listen to how he was talking to me. I was not one of his friends who was going to go and kill myself. I was not some baby. I think I know how to take care of myself by now.

Let's try and get some sleep.

Again, he tries to lay me back down on the bed.

You're so tense. Lie back.

I slip back on the boxer shorts on the floor, knowing I've already shown myself once to have too many dumb feelings.

He thought these boxer shorts were sexy. They were a present. He gave them to me when I got here.

There's no way I can leave. I have to be rational about how there's nowhere for me to really go from here.

From him comes another relax. Just relax.

He pulls me to him while I start breaking down, admit I want to go home.

He knows. He knows.

He tells me to go to sleep.

I can't think of anything good.

I don't want to cry in front of him. I've already shown him how lost I get with him in a room like this. I wanted him to tell me a story, a story about when he was younger. I wanted to hear about when he was little.

You know his scar? When he was a kid, there was this brick wall, and he thought he could bust it down with a baseball bat. He just kept hitting it, and then this happened.

The next morning I have to show him somehow what happened last night is not going to happen again. That's what I know he wants to see, to be sure he's not going to have to put up with all that ever again, that there aren't going to be anymore outbursts like that. That's not something he should expect from me. He didn't like it when I lost control of myself and headed for my bag, threatening to walk out on him into Los Angeles, hysterical, leaving the hotel room.

Where will you go? Where do you plan on going if you leave here, he asked.

I'm sorry, I apologize, I'm sorry I lost control of myself last night. It won't happen again.

He lies on the pillow beside me, trying to look relieved.

I was like some sort of emotional explosion.

You know that? I mean, what do you think last night was really about?

What does he mean?

I mean, it wasn't about the rubber, was it?

Then what was it about? I don't know what he's looking for from me.

Only you can answer this question. Do you think you might be in love with me? Do you think that's what last night was really about?

I'd never wanted to tell him I'd been trying to fall in love with him.

He says, You know it's hard for me to ask. He wants me to recognize that. But he feels it's important we talk about it, figure this all out. I mean, he knows I already think he's some sort of egomaniac and all. It's very hard for him to ask me this question.

I don't know how he's defining love, exactly.

In the bed I turn my back to him, stare at the wall I ran towards last night.

My bag is on the floor of the closet in the room in the hotel. I can see that. If I left the room, I'd walk down a hall, past the bathroom where he showered last night after it all went wrong.

There was a nice white carpet throughout the room, except for the kitchen area off the hall after the bathroom.

Then the hall opened up into the living room area where there was a couch, a table room service put the tray down on. Every morning that week there was orange juice and cappuccino in white thick porcelain, nice bread and butter, slices of fruit, if we wanted it.

I was dumb enough after only six or so months of knowing him to then ask him if he thought he loved me.

He didn't know. He didn't know what he felt for me.

He's being honest. I can tell by the way there's no conviction in the tone of his voice. I can tell he's been asked this before, many times. It sounds like he's rehearsed his answer.

I know in the movies, he says, I would just say I love you, too, no problem, and we would fall down into each other's arms.

He stops to search for some further, implausible scenario he thinks I'm imagining. I'm not. I get up out of the bed and go to get my bag. I know I have no money, no knowledge of the place. I don't care. I know I've never been here before, but I want to get away from him, that's all.

I want to know why he brought me here. I don't get it. I don't get why he wants me to say I love him just so he can say he doesn't love me.

I know he's not going to say he loves me.

I tell him I have no delusions, none, none whatsoever, about what I mean to him, what I've ever meant to him, or what we did together. I say not anymore.

He pulls me back to the king-sized bed, the white sheets and white blanket and white pillows, away from my bag of clothes that haven't been washed since the last time I had enough money to do laundry. Inside that bag his coat is folded all up.

You've gotta stop it. Just stop it.

He says it gently, but his arms are holding me very tightly like something he wants to break. I know he doesn't want to have to answer to my getting lost here. Everyone down in the lobby would see me like that, then, leaving here.

If I just tell him where I plan on going he'll let me go.

I want to know what he feels for me.

I don't know if I love you.

He really doesn't.

He lets me go.

He doesn't know what it feels like. He has no idea what it's supposed to feel like.

I wanted to tell him you never know, that you just have to believe it, believe that you are.

That's how it starts happening, that's how you have to let it start happening.

I promise what happened last night will never happen again. I will never let it happen again.

He asks if I mean we're never going to have sex again.

I loved having sex with him.

Something goes off in his head, you know? When he sees himself going down a certain road, towards hurt and problems. It tells him to stop and turn, but this time he doesn't think he should, not with me.

He doesn't think he should turn away.

He wanted me to leave there with good memories.

What's in Front of Him

At dinner I'm a boy there with him. There are about thirty other people in our party at the table, and the dinner is being thrown by a man who is known as the King of Switzerland.

The King of Switzerland has not one, but two boys with him. There's one on either side. They don't speak much English. Mostly they smile and pick at course after course, they seem to know their places, appear at ease with how they fit into this whole room. Nobody ever really knows who the boys are. They don't expect it to come up.

It's somewhere between dessert and what comes next. The boys don't seem at all threatened, when before the elderberry sorbet is brought out, the King of Switzerland appears to be flirting with me. It's not so much his foot under the table, but his eyes directly across it. My boyfriend seems glad someone else seems so taken with me, that it's not just him.

The King of Switzerland tells me I should come visit him anytime, anytime I want, if I ever come back to Switzerland. If I ever find myself back here again, look him up.

Thanks.

He takes a moment to carefully peel the label off a bottle of dessert wine older than me, gives me the label as my informal passport, proof of this exclusive citizenship, bestowed by him, says he thought I might like a souvenir. He doesn't let the year of the wine go unremarked, either.

Sixty-nine is a good number, oui? He thinks he's just made a clever joke. It might have been funnier in French.

He tells us Napoleon once ate in this very room.

Really?

My boyfriend talks to someone else at the table. He tells me the wine costs a thousand dollars a bottle, that I better enjoy it. Everyone laughs at something I didn't quite catch. I try to concentrate fully on the seaweed on my plate in front of me. One of the boys with the King tries to say something to me, but I don't understand through his accent, so I just nod yeah to whatever. I'm thinking about what my boyfriend brought up earlier when he asked me if I trusted him. I knew he meant whether or not I believe he cheats on me when he goes away on his trips to Paris or wherever, business. There was something he just wanted to get off his chest before dinner.

I said yes, I trusted him.

He only brings it up because there was something he felt like he had to tell me. Last time he was in Paris, that last time, he kissed a model. It was nothing. It was no big deal, he says. He just thought he should tell me.

I didn't know who the model was, since I try not to pay attention to these kinds of things. He repeats it was nothing.

He just felt like he should tell me, said he only did it because she really needed the kiss from him. He laughed and called her a tart, like it's all just some joke, said the model was really depressed. She's having a lot of problems with her boyfriend, so she needed to turn to mine. He's a London celebrity, her boyfriend, some big deal.

Since she's a model, everyone knew they were a couple.

High-profile, my boyfriend says up in our room.

She was crushed. The British tabloids ran a story about how her famous boyfriend was obviously cheating on her with another famous woman, right in front of her face, with someone who supposedly is not even attractive, like my boyfriend tells me the model is attractive.

My boyfriend's high-profile here, too, in London, all over the world. He makes certain deals.

The model was devastated. She didn't know where to turn. She turned to my boyfriend. I mean, they were in Paris together.

She's coming to dinner tonight, if her flight into Switzerland arrives on time. She was planning on coming to Switzerland anyway.

Everyone at the table is curious, buzzed on the prospect of her and the sixty-nine wine.

I keep trying to look like I belong here, like I know my place. If I couldn't quite understand the level of conversation, maybe I'd be more inclined to just enjoy the meal, like the King's boys. Everyone else speaks fluent English but them. Occasionally the King translates something for them. Someone at the table asks my boyfriend about the model again.

You guys are friends, right? When is she arriving?

We finish the main course. Still no model.

Everyone waits with bated breath, digesting the evening. The King of Switzerland brushes my knee under the table while my boyfriend goes deep into another conversation next to me. I'm still here.

Back at the hotel, earlier up in the room, I didn't want him to think it bothered me that he kissed her, so I lied. I told him I had a confession to make, too.

OK. He looked at me like he didn't believe me. But, OK.

Remember Philippe?

Yeah?

I kissed him.

He makes a little sound like he's truly disgusted. Then he asks me if my mouth was open or closed.

I don't say my thoughts exactly. At least Philippe's not a model.

My boyfriend reminds me she's a supermodel. Besides, they were both really drunk.

Kind of like that first night he ever kissed me. He was really drunk then, too.

He tells me she knows all about me. I don't know what she could possibly know. That I'm this boy he saw out dancing one night when he was trying to be not quite so high-profile?

He trusted I'd noticed him. I had. We went back to where I sleep in the kitchen. He was home from some trips. I knew he had something to do with this clothing company. He knew I'd slept with one of his loyal, old friends. He figured he couldn't go too wrong with me, with giving himself to me. If I was good enough for his friend I was good enough for him.

I'm supposed to be looking forward to meeting her at dinner like everyone else.

Up in our room, in between kissing me, he says she really

wants to meet me, that she's really looking forward to it. We'd all be together in Switzerland.

This was our vacation, I don't say.

He thinks she's curious to see what kind of man could snag him.

Perhaps that would have been the time to press upon him I've never really been so sure I do have him, object, I mean, sure he sleeps with me whenever he's around, but what does that make me when he's not around?

I don't know what he tells other people, like her.

She arrives some time after we've finished the main course and just before dessert. The old dishes are cleared to make way for new, smaller ones. We've been expecting her. Everybody knows who she is. Nobody seems to mind she's just now getting here. She's probably always late to such sorts of things.

My boyfriend stands to introduce her, like here she is everyone.

He proudly says her name, kisses her on the cheek, practically places her up on the table and twirls her. Everyone keeps looking at her, me, then him.

She looks down at the floor, affecting half-abashed, and says she hopes she's not too late.

I choke on an imaginary bone. No, not at all. We've just finished the main course.

She smiles for the camera, everyone's eyes in the room. Cheese? The waiters enter the ornate wood room with more silver plates.

Oh, yes, you have cheese here before dessert. She models her poise.

Everyone hears him ask her if she already checked into the hotel. She smiles, has. I notice he doesn't lower his voice when he talks to her like he does with me.

As far as the room is concerned, I might as well be one of the boys with the King now. Maybe some of them do think that's why I'm there, for the King, all the King's friends.

She takes my boyfriend's hand, wants to be close to him so he can hold her hand through this difficult time. He finally turns to me because I haven't risen with everyone else at the table. I don't want to grab her hand. He wanted to point me out, before she moves down to where the tiny white place card with her clearly printed name is seated, at the other end of the table, thankfully. My boyfriend offers to walk her across the room, but first he tells her who I am, the boy he's fucking.

The King smiles. The other boys nibble brie.

I am in love with him. I am quiet about my feelings for him, for fear of showing any of my many desperations out loud. It's all a part of an unspoken contract between us.

I'm the one he's been telling her about. I'm pursuing an English degree off somewhere. I keep him slight company when there's nothing more important like a movie opening or a fashion show. Switzerland seemed like the ideal place for a spring break.

She looks at my boyfriend like they really need to talk. Not now, but later.

Oh yeah. That's me. She's forgotten my name because she's better with faces.

My boyfriend walks her down to her chair, kisses her again on the cheek.

He's so glad to see her here. It's been days since they were both in Paris together. The King takes this small opportunity to turn to me and confess.

I was the first person in Switzerland to have a waterbed. Do you like waterbeds?

The boys smile.

She comes back down to where he and I are trying to act normal. She wants a quick cigarette before dessert. People are shuffling around, getting up to look closer at the paintings on the walls, come over and smile at her, or nod from a distance, when she catches their eyes engrossed.

After rolling her a cigarette with his loose tobacco, he holds up a light.

The King of Switzerland asks why I don't smoke.

She turns to me, exhales. What did you get for Valentine's Day?

I look pointedly at my boyfriend and the opportunity he has just given me. He forgot. Thanks. I don't want her trying to make conversation with me, though.

A card, I lie.

My boyfriend reminds me he called me.

Oh yeah, that's right.

She got roses from some young actor they both know. Imagine that.

She asks me when I'm leaving France.

Classes start back Wednesday.

I must be excited if this my first time in Switzerland. The whole table watches her talk to me and my boyfriend. She notices, smiles yet again, says look. She's ready to perform if we are ready to watch. She takes the napkin still in my boyfriend's lap and turns the white cloth into a crude approximation of a penis, sculpts intently with her dainty hands, becomes a makeshift shaft artist right before our very eyes, laughs.

One of the husbands applauds.

I want to know if she learned that in modeling school, but before I can even clear my throat she begins telling sex jokes she is the punch line of. The men eat her up. My boyfriend grins. If I'm not mistaking, even the King is momentarily riveted.

73

She's charming. She's a model. It's her job.

Never one to be pegged, though, she would like to take this opportunity to tell us one day she's going to give it all up for photography. She photographs everywhere she goes, takes pictures of all the other models around her. She thinks they're so beautiful.

Don't you think so?

She looks at my boyfriend, and then she tells us she really wants to have a baby.

My boyfriend is on the phone in our room with one of his friends, telling him about all the problems the model is unfortunately having. She's going to see a doctor about getting some antidepressants.

He gets off the phone, tells his friend he'll call back later tonight or first thing tomorrow morning. He wants to know if I think we should ask her over.

She's right down the hall, all alone in her room. She did say earlier over dinner she had some pictures of Budapest she really wanted to show him.

Do I resent her being here?

I try to articulate with my eyes how insensitive I think it was of her to come when this was supposed to be our time together. He doesn't get it, so I ask how come she can bring her problems to him and I'm expected to be fine all the time? He knows I can't afford antidepressants.

I say she's going to become dependent on some doctor. I want to know what's going to happen once my boyfriend is not around for her? Then what's she going to do?

I don't want her expecting him to solve her problems.

She knows all about us. She knows how much I mean to him. She likes me. She said at dinner she thought I was very sensitive.

This is a tactic to get me to be nice to her because she supposedly noticed me.

So?

I just wanted you to like her. I just wanted you to think I have interesting people for friends.

Oh.

It doesn't matter what I think because tomorrow she's going to have breakfast with us, and then we are all going to go shopping together, or I can stay at the hotel.

Besides, I should be glad. She said I was very intense.

He brings her up to the room before she goes. He wanted to give her a chance to say goodbye. She has decided to go. He's been downstairs helping her with her bags. There will be no shopping today.

He jokes he wants to see us hug in front of him.

I notice immediately she doesn't quite know how to compose herself in my arms, since she knows I'm not interested in anything about her appearance.

Bye, I say, pulling away.

She's leaving.

She says maybe we'll see each other again. Soon.

Yeah. Have a safe trip, I say, knowing now what she's shown me. He has other things to look forward to when I'm not there.

Blake's

I was invited to vacation with his family. They were going to go to the beach at Tybee Island this time, and then on to Savannah, where the movie based on that book was about to start shooting. This book had made Savannah a popular tourists' spot of late, and this was one of the reasons his mom wanted to go, too. She wanted to see it.

Before that though, we were taking his nephew to the Island to see the ocean for the first time in his life.

Locations all around us were being scouted.

By this time, we have already stopped touching. But none of his family knows yet. He was seeing this psychiatrist, about what might be wrong with him. I was surely part of it, how needy I'd grown with him, how demanding I was getting. He was told by the psychiatrist to stop touching me for a while. He said that if I loved him, I'd wait.

I'd grown impatient.

When his mom invited me on the trip with them, she had no

idea. They hadn't figured it out yet, about him and me. He hadn't told any of them I was no longer a part of this part of his life.

If I wanted to come, I should come, he said. He wasn't going to stop me. I have my own selfish reasons for wanting to go, follow through with the proposed trip. I knew we would still share a bed. That's just the type of man he was. Anything else would be too awkward to bring up right now, just then, when we were supposed to be having a good time.

I would be reminded, like I always am, of things that have already happened with him, like that time he took me to London, another vacation with his family, and I was so anxious arriving I was upset instantly when I saw the hotel staff at Blake's had separated us, given me and him a room with two single beds, I guess since we were both men. Joking that night, he asked which bed I wanted, not seeing how upset I was.

He assured me I was the only person he'd ever brought to London, that he hadn't brought me there for nothing. We did curl as close as if one body wrapped around itself, despite the inevitable separation coming, the morning at the end of the week, when the vacation was over.

He and his family were going on to Dublin next. They watched him as he coaxed me towards the waiting cab, told me I should put my sunglasses on, to cover up how I didn't want to go. They could see. He watched me hug his mom, as his face glowed. The nephew, just a baby then, said goodbye with awkward, silent waves. He couldn't stand yet. The two dads there shook my hand. Sisters hugged me. It was his entire extended family.

I felt guilty for being a boy, but he kissed me goodbye in front of all of them, even the driver, then.

We drove up to Savannah separately from his family, to join them at the hotel. The vacation was already in progress. We were a few hours later starting out. I watched the clock on the dashboard for almost the whole, silent ride. I didn't want to ruin this illusion of us at peace, yet.

In the hotel, I was right. We share a bed, but it's in a double room with his younger sister and the guy she's still sleeping with. In the bed across from them, we don't touch. He stays behind at the hotel with the older members of the family, his parents, his older sister and her husband, while I go to a bar to have a drink, eat a salad with the younger sister and the guy she sleeps with. I want to make the most of the vacation, even though he says he doesn't know why I've come.

When I first started feeling him slip away, because of what the psychiatrist was telling him to do, when I could no longer reassure each of us nightly that we brought something to each other, I expressed doubts to some friends we had. One husband was Moroccan, who didn't find it implausible that I thought a curse had been placed on me, that I feared it. He told me I should go to the beach at high tide, swim out in the sea in my clothes, dunk myself under seven successive waves and then turn, swim back to shore, dropping the clothes from my body, changing into fresh ones I should have brought along, never once looking back. I don't know why I never did any of this.

We stay together on the Island in a beach house his parents rent, large enough for everyone and me. He and I are going to take the back bedroom, because the knots he's got in his neck from all his stress require special attention. That's where the better bed appears to be. There are enough rooms for everyone. He rolls over in the night, tells me not to touch him, asks me why I even came, why I think I'm there. I knew I was asking for it.

I sit on the beach with his family. They are running out to meet all the waves.

I have a disposable camera with me, so I'm trying to take as many pictures as I can, mainly of him when he isn't looking.

No one knew who he was on this Island, who I was, but it didn't matter. We recognized the story. We'd all heard it before, in one version or another.

On the way back home, we all stop to go antique shopping before turning onto the highway. His car is going to follow his parents' and siblings' cars.

I wait outside while he and his family all hunt souvenirs inside. There's a gazing ball. My face shows up there in it. These mirrored globes were originally made for gardens, yards, his mom tells me when they all come out of the store and see me looking at it. The evil spirits, ghosts, would see how ugly they looked showing up and then hopefully be scared away.

The Heart of Paris

I departed alone. I arrived from Luxembourg by train in Paris. Again, I had to change my money. The different currencies went through my hands as I tried to ask for directions. The train I was looking for, to London, the one that goes under the sea, departs from Gare de l'Est. I finally made this out in the French I don't quite speak.

I'm told I need to get on the local subway where I am at Gare du Nord, take it one stop to Gare de l'Est where I should be.

Sliding into the silver train, I shoot forward to the next pause, before the train goes on again. I carry all of my baggage with me.

Eyes occasionally look me up and down.

At Gare de l'Est, I run up the stairs. From Luxembourg there's been a time change, and I'm too late to make the last train to London tonight. The next train is at six in the morning. That leaves me with ten hours to stand around in the cold. I have a hundred franc note left to my name, and nowhere to go tonight. I was going to go to my sister in London, call her whenever I got there. I never have any money, but I'm not going to let that stop me. It will be an adventure, that's what I originally thought. I said I'd be fine until I got there.

Gare de l'Est is an open air train station.

The November winds make the cement floor ice black.

Cold steam seems to pour out of my mouth. I'm scared of spending my last bit of money trying to figure out somewhere to possibly go on the subway. At least in London there would be someone I could ask for help, if I was lost, further directions I could understand. I can't figure out how to call my sister or any-one from here, how to make the phones work. The French speak their French. I'm stuck here for tonight.

More and more families run off to the street lit with neon out-side. I eye expensive cheese sandwiches, and finally I break my bill for a late croissant and coffee for dinner, before the concession stands call it quits. The platforms keep emptying out, thinning to a few lost souls. Trains stand still. Fewer bodies walk around fewer bodies. Movement dwindles to the occasional man walking the station from one end to the other.

The toilets here require coins. Hot showers are also available there on the lower level, if you have money for the slots that open them. I have no credit card, nothing, in case of some emergency.

I thought I'd be fine, that I'd just get to London and take it from there, call my sister once I got there.

I shove my hands deep down into the worn pockets of my jeans. The few men left in the station are gathering around a glowing pillar of sorts, a column of electricity that emits heat. Their mouths mumble in this or that language I don't really know, but I understand at least how their bodies are drawn to the radiation of warmth in the center of the station's body. We all understand what it's like to be cold.

I walk over and stand around with them for a couple of hours, alternating between sitting down on my suitcase and standing up to stretch my legs, letting the blood course downward.

A few more men warm their hands around the pillar, reaching out as far as they dare before pulling back, voicing half-hearted observations, like it's only four more hours.

Before the station opens back up properly, they mean, and the trains start running again. People will flood the gates, push against these entries to the veins of the city.

Only four more hours to wait, like this.

When I could take no more of just standing there like I was, I figured it would cost nothing to wander the streets until the sun rose. It couldn't be any colder.

I started to walk out towards the street, and that's when he followed me, beyond the arches, through the western wing. Why else would I have been here in the middle of the night, this late? He must have been able to see I had nowhere to go. He began to converse with me in broken English. I used versions of my few French phrases. He knew I didn't understand much more than his hand on my arm.

He followed me down rue Saint-Martin, further into the city that was closing in around itself. He looked like any other unattractive man. Only a few lights still shined in windows without shades like open eyes watching us wander. Paris did sleep.

He was following me.

He was trying to find a way to phrase desire to find a bed with me. The streets watched. The other men warmed their hands as they watched him come after me. They did nothing. It was the district of the working class. I wondered if he thought I lived here. He kept following me, trying to translate a desire. It was hard to understand exactly what he wanted. I didn't know where I was going, not really. I was just walking.

I just kept walking. I'd never been with a man before in Paris.

I don't know what he thinks of me, if he thinks I come here, sneak out in the middle of the nights, to wander down around the train platforms, despite the baggage, looking for someone like he does. I stare at him, thinking at first maybe he's just trying to ask me for money.

D'argent.

He could be offering it to me. That could be it, part of it. Or is he just cold, homeless, his desire simple? Does he think I have a floor to offer him, anything?

Taxis yawn by us. I don't know how to ask him what he wants. Does he live close by? He has greater access to my body in this weather. I have nowhere to sleep tonight. The thin coat of my racing jacket is so beside the point.

I'd been standing around outside in the air of that station so long, desiring more warmth the later it got, waiting for the night to finally end. That's it. I was turning more tolerant towards any and all company the longer I stood in it.

He's saying he'll buy a room for me tonight, for us.

That's what he's saying. All I have to do is go with him. I don't like him but he'll help. He rubs up and down the length of my racing jacket, black, with the red stripe up the sleeve, while the buildings watch and promise their privacy.

He could push me up against one of the many locked doors up and down the street. He leads me down an alley, and I follow, thinking he must have some cheap hotel in mind, something. He fondles my biceps as he leads me, smiling. I weakly smile back. He offers to help me carry my luggage. It's heavy. I'm a little afraid he's going to run off with it. I don't know why I have a hard-on, but now I do. I'm sure he can see it. He reaches down to touch it then, running his fingers up and down the vein of my jeans. The gold teeth of my zipper strain a little more under his fingers prying.

He's anyone, French. My mouth knows how he's about to get to me, as soon as he finds a place dark enough in me, for me. The situation is suddenly deep enough to go ahead and concede.

The first hotel won't give him a single rate for us, even if there is only one bed we'd sleep on top of each other in.

There are two of you, a desk clerk clicks, wanting more francs.

The man decides to take me someplace cheaper.

Going from one run-down hotel to another in the vicinity, I lug my suitcase behind him holding out this promise of the small comfort of a bed. He might give me some money, which I need. I had just enough money to get to London. It's been a day since I've slept. Maybe I won't really have to do anything, just be allowed to sleep, share the bed with him. He could be nice to me. It's been two days straight now I've been traveling, trying to sleep sitting up on trains.

Once he gets us far enough away from the station, tracks, I'm aware that he could do whatever he wants. There must have been other boys like me he's followed before, trying to read their thoughts, their wants, their needs, standing around the station.

I look like another.

Gare de l'Est is the name of the street.

Another desk clerk in another hotel looks at us. Another desk clerk makes an assessment, quotes some price reasonable enough for the man to pay. There's our room key.

Up the stairs and inside, the bed in the chamber is no larger than a padded bench. He touches my knee on it when I sit down. I smile like it's a pleasant day.

He motions for me to get naked. Get up and get naked. He is undressing, standing there wanting me up against the wall in the room we've parked in.

Now that it's started, I don't know how not to do it.

Outside, Paris breathes through all its cells.

There's no shade on the window. Here's the night's warmth, criminal. The lights from the street break through the window as he huddles with me behind it, turning him towards something more golden.

Later, he unwraps a candy bar he's brought along, and he starts feeding me the foreign chocolate. It might be something they do here I don't know about. The chocolate has been wrapped up by him in a piece of newspaper colored like monopoly money.

He sucks on my bottom lip while I chew, tells me to touch him here and here. I want to sleep now, but I'm not going any-where that fast. He wants me to eat more chocolate. He keeps shoving it in my mouth.

He wants me to be a plane on top of him, a ship under him.

He pretends like he's strangling me and I don't say anything, just lie still and pretend he's just pretending. I try to drift away from him in my mind, here, now, and forever.

Someone's touching me. It's nobody.

He looks like nothing.

Chemicals flood my brain, beat out memories of every mouth I've ever encountered like this. He is none of them. He's nothing.

This is nothing.

All of them, I thought I loved all of them before him.

He is something else, something new, and something nothing. I have to tell myself this is still me, here.

He lights his cigarette, and though it strikes me as odd, it's happening. He begins to ash the cigarette into my hair. He sticks his tongue into my mouth now, and his skin smells like suffocation, feels smooth like nothing but a rock, a rubbed blank subway token.

It's Paris, and we are here for only one night.

In London I'll see my sister. That's where she lives. It was almost Christmas. She will be surprised to see me, finally.

He wants me to swallow him in my mouth, now, like coal.

I can feel my body again, but he is putting his hands around my neck. He is putting more of the chocolate in my mouth again.

In a flash, he holds his big hands around my neck. He's just playing like he's strangling me. He says something about me in French. He tastes the chocolate in my mouth, melting.

The room is warm.

Outside, it was so cold I was turning purple. He wants me again, awake. He shakes me, lights another cigarette, reminds me he's still in the room with me, reminds me where I am.

I'm in Paris, waiting for the train in the morning.

Later, he starts to snore, and I do get to sleep finally, up against the wall I could crawl into, like I could crawl inside the building's foundation.

86

In the morning, he won't let me walk back to the train station alone.

I want him to let me go. He won't let me leave. We stumble back while the sky is still mostly dark around its edges, bruised in its own way.

Some of the men from last night are still there in the station, still waiting on their missed trains. He offers to buy me a coffee. I think that's what he asks me if I want. I nod, but then I'm more reluctant realizing that means we have to go back across the street together. Nothing is open yet at the station but the doors.

There's an all hours cafe across the street. It was there all along.

I was distracted. I was scared I was going to miss my train if I didn't just stand right there and wait for it. I was planning to sleep the whole way under the sea, through the Chunnel.

We cross the street together, and there inside the cafe is a boy who nods his head coyly at me, points out the waiter while the door comes to rest closed behind me, telling me to have a seat, explaining with his hands that I could join him.

3

The Island

The pizza place on the corner where I'm going underground is closed. It's too late at night. I've made little bargains with myself, that's how apprehensive I am. If I get a call before from someone else, I won't go. If I get there and the schedule of the ferry doesn't coincide, I won't go. If I have to wait too long, I won't go. If the two boys beside me on the wooden bench seem interested in me, or approach me, then I will stay here with them. I will follow them off wherever.

My stomach is empty.

I wondered what kind of man would call for me, want me this late at night, to come all the way out there to him.

He called again, insistent. He wanted to see if I was still planning on coming.

Yeah, I said, but, I tried to talk myself out of it.

Well, since I was already on my way, I might as well do it, he said. Come on out. It's across the water. He'll meet me at the ramp where you pick up passengers getting off the ferry. He'll pick me up in his car.

Where do I live? Where again? Where exactly?

I tell him the name of the area, the hill, what two places he might recognize it's between, but he didn't know it. He offered to figure out some way to get me back home, after he was done with me. It would be late, if I was even still counting the hours by then. This all took place over the phone. I might still be there.

What was I wearing? I should tell him, so he'll be able to spot me.

That way he'll be able to recognize me, since he's never seen me before. He'll be able to pick me out, to pick me up.

I told him I'd be wearing a big blue coat, a red sock hat. I was white.

Some people were not waiting for the boat. Some were crazy, keeping themselves company. Some talked to themselves, looked in trash cans. Some fell asleep on the wooden benches there in the station. Some were there just to sleep.

I bought a piece of bread I couldn't really taste, waiting for the next ferry, watching the pigeons that still flew in and walked around on the waiting room floor, in the middle of the night, early, early morning.

The green necks of the birds and their heads bobbed, even this late at night, this early in the morning.

The boat was moving now, the ferry gliding out past the dock.

I was on the boat.

I saw the Statue for the first time. I'd lived here now for about half a year and this was the first time I'd ever seen it. This was home to liberty. I fixed my eyes on the rising that disappeared for one second moving through the chop of black waves under us, the boat. I was forgetting everything I'd known.

Then it reemerged, closer up.

I saw two lights this time, the one in her hand and the one over her head, inside the crown.

21, Compositions

picture 1

I was the fair haired one, the only one. The other two boys had darker hair, black, brown. One of them was skinny, like me, even a little more, and the other guy was built, but still looked young-ish, cute. That had something to do with his ears and tentative smile, big and kind of goofy.

There were three brown bottles of beer on the table in front of us, our bodies already angled slightly cocky in wooden chairs like one might expect to find in a dorm room we are supposedly in. My hand is wrapped around the width of one of the cold bottles. Moist labels will be blurred. We're not here to sell beer.

The guy with muscles shows the skinny boy his hand and I'm laughing in this picture like this is just how I've decided to spend some boring weekend. You can see the dimple in my left cheek.

We boys have been told by the other men in the room,

the photographer and his boyfriend, the art director, to enjoy all the beer we like, drink as much as we like. There's lots more. I should be pacing myself, though. It doesn't take much to get me drunk.

The photographer and his boyfriend the art director live here in this large loft. They work out of where they've built a set for us. They want it to look like we are off at college in a dorm. The art director is particularly proud of the walls he's plastered with glossy photos of women's spread legs, their fingers dug in, and nipples erect on huge breasts. We all laugh at the inside joke, how ridiculous it all is, how none of us are even remotely interested in that. Between the women, the art director has carefully placed a couple of guys, pretty harmless images pulled out of skateboarding magazines and such, a couple of pros with shirts off to sweat better, a few muscle men any guy would be willing to let another see on his walls, nothing like you'll see us doing in front of them.

There's a particular picture I will come back to during all of this, just for myself, while sitting at the table, waiting to be turned on. The ad is of a group of guys huddled around together, backs to camera, looking down at whatever happens to be sticking out in front of each, in a circle they've made with their bodies, gauging I suppose respective size and length.

Our night will one day be kept under mattresses, on top shelves of closets, behind sweaters, safe away from wives and the prying eyes of girlfriends. But some men will share this issue with various, more open partners.

The art director notices I'm not really touching my beer and asks me if he can get me anything else to drink.

I'll take some water.

We have orange juice, too.

Water's fine.

Are you sure?

OK, I'll take some orange juice.

Then, since I'm hungry, they order-in sushi, their treat. Of course none of this ends up present in the picture, wouldn't really fit the overall mood. The other two guys nurse their beers, aren't really hungry. We size each other up sweetly, while the photographer and his boyfriend the art director are talking about how to make the scene ring even more true.

We were just about to get started. The guy with muscles asked me and the skinny boy if either of us had ever done this before. The skinny boy hadn't.

The guy with muscles is nervous, even though he's done it a couple of times before.

He says to me I don't seem nervous at all.

I tell him I've modeled for some art classes before, back in college.

That was before I moved to the city. It was different, though. For the art classes, you had to try not to get hard in front of the students there to draw you. Tonight is just the opposite. The point is to capture us three getting and getting each other stiff, proceeding from there accordingly in flashes.

picture 2

The guy with muscles wins a round, so the skinny guy removes a sock. It looks like I'm reaching under the table to do something similar. Shoes are already off. The guy with muscles shuffles the cards for the next hand, smiling.

I had to go out and buy underwear for tonight. The art director told me over the phone he wanted me to bring both briefs and boxers. He'd tell me what I was going to wear when I got there, depending on what the other two boys brought.

We all look about eighteen, although none of us are that young still.

picture 3

The guy with muscles tells me I look like a little cat, when I tip the big blue porcelain bowl the art director poured the miso into, from the plastic, up to my lips. The picture doesn't show this, though, or that our beers have been replaced by the art director, after the other skinny boy finished off my first.

This guy with muscles removes his black tank top because someone else has won the round. I'm already forgetting rules given quickly to me at the beginning of the game.

You can't show actual penetration in the magazine the shoot is for. We can't show our three dicks in each other's hands, only our own. We can place them however suggestively near certain areas we like, though, make due. What we do between takes, the photographer says reloading film, as his boyfriend moves around props, and places an economy pack of Kleenex beside the bed we'll be moving onto by the end of the night, is up to us, totally.

The main thing is to have fun, the photographer clicks his camera.

I soon know I'll be the first one to lose all my clothes. I'm not a good card player.

We've switched to 21 because the poker hands were taking too long and the others are still mostly dressed. The other skinny boy goes out to smoke on the fire escape, after telling me I've got a dancer's body. He has a friend who tours with a dance company. He could give me his number if I'm interested.

At the end of the night, the photographer will give us a number, and all three of us boys will exchange digits as well. Once outside the loft, the skinny boy and the guy with muscles appear to walk off the same way, but I won't join them.

picture 4

Soon we have to get hard for the pictures. The photographer tells the other skinny boy he should start trying to do something about working himself up first. You can't really see in the pictures the scar on the side of the other skinny boy's face. It's from a car wreck. Earlier he wanted to change chairs with me at the table from where the art director originally wanted him, to turn to the camera his better half.

He has to take off his pants now. He jokes he keeps getting moist. He means little spots of pre-cum that dot the white cotton of his jockeys, making them close to translucent in spots where his dick presses up against the fabric, in the shape of readiness. Before these pictures are sent off to the magazine, we will all come over to the photographer's house again, look at all the prints. We can say if there are any we really don't like.

Ones that show his scar won't be used.

picture 5

The other skinny boy keeps pushing up under his white jockeys, trying hard to stand up straight. There are the nice black hairs along the inside of his thighs, as he sits in a chair, with his hands on his knees, waiting for the guy with muscles to deal again, another hand.

We are still before the table, while the guy with muscles shuffles.

picture 6

I lose my shirt but am asked to keep the tie knotted around my neck. It trails down the center of my now bare chest.

picture 7

The other skinny boy, like he just can't help it, sits there and feels like touching it. We look like just a bunch of guys around a table, possibly friends. What's it matter if we see one of us horny?

The other skinny boy pinches himself lightly. I've lost my pants and taken off the tie. The boy with muscles is wearing a jockstrap. The two guys behind the scenes are still fully dressed. The skinny boy wants to light the prop joint on the table. The art director rubs through his jeans himself.

The photographer tells me I'm gorgeous, god, that he really feels likes he's getting this through his camera. He tells me I should get hard. The art director asks if he can help. My hand is against my face in the close-up. I say, oh, all right.

We play like we're just joking around, not like he's really going to get down there in front of me on the floor, in front of his boyfriend behind the camera, place a face between my thighs, nuzzle around first with his chin, then tongue, take me in inch by inch in and out of his mouth. He does, though.

The art director looks up steadily into my face while he's doing it. I hang out his mouth more and more pointedly.

picture 8

The other skinny boy is told to slide down his white jockey shorts now, while the guy with muscles looks on. The subtext is supposedly I've lost the next round of strip 21, and I have to go over to the other skinny boy's chair to go down on him.

We are no longer really playing.

According to the *Encyclopedia of Sexual Perversions* the photographer read from to us earlier at the start of the night, once a player runs out of clothes, the player has to continue bartering with sexual favors winners specify.

picture 9

The other skinny boy bends over to pull down his jockeys, a drained bottle of beer in front of him on the table.

picture 10

On the floor on my knees, in front of the other skinny boy back down in his chair, it's time for me to get ready to put my head down in the lap. The guy with muscles is asked to stand out from behind the table, so we can all see he's ready, too.

picture 11

I move up to kiss the skinny boy's neck, while the guy with muscles crosses closer.

We touch ourselves during the process, while the voice behind the camera directs us not to stop.

picture 12

The skinny guy's dick is pressed against my ear, the shaft rested on my shoulder, as I'm kneeling again. The guy with muscles stands close enough to put his hand on my back, begin bending to go down near us, his dick brushing against the top of my hair, head, blonde.

picture 13

We are moved over to the prop bed. The other skinny boy is glad he had a shot of liquor and a beer, then another, and a joint, before he came over tonight. He looks on, on his knees behind the joined bodies of me and the guy with muscles kissing. The guy with muscles is on top of me, his tongue wanting me, his lips riding over my face.

My hand clenches the back of his neck, like I want to pull him into me. He asks me quietly if I mind if he takes me in his mouth for real. The photographer takes a picture of the moment just before.

I open my eyes and look at the guy with muscles over me. He looks like an old friend of mine. I kiss his face, keep thinking this is really something. The skinny boy comes over like he's told, to help me lose myself further, my face hidden against his neck while my body feels him out.

I'm barely aware we're being seen like this now. I feel the skin up and down the skinny boy's back, sliding my hand around to his chest, spread over his skin, flushing.

The photographer walks over to join us and arrange a new position, put me behind the other skinny boy up on his knees, and tells me to throw back my head, to stretch my neck just like I'm about to come. I think I hear a couple of actual sighs, the pleasure of exhaling in this pressure.

picture 14

I slid my body off the bed so just the back of my head rests on the edge of it, as they arch over my upturned face. My hand reaches up like I'm about to just start grabbing whoever.

picture 15

Back on my back on the bed with the guy with muscles between my legs, and the skinny guy behind him, it's supposed to look like the skinny boy is fucking the guy with muscles, while the guy with muscles kisses me.

picture 16

The skinny boy and me on our knees are approaching the guy with muscles.

He has his pick.

picture 17

While they kneel on either side of me, they arch over my stomach, their dicks pointing at and wanting each other. The guy with muscles reaches over me to pinch the nipple of the skinny guy.

picture 18

Just a simple close-up of my hand, palm-down, low on my stomach, the fingers spread to support my dick arching across my knuckles.

You can see my thighs spread wide.

picture 19

I laugh with my teeth and nose against a stomach.

There's a hand on my shoulder in the frame.

picture 20

We have our arms around each other, are about to get photographed getting dressed again.

picture 21

The centerfold is the two of them on top of me.

The skinny guy's ass arches as he slides up over onto the back of the guy with muscles, who's on his stomach underneath, on top of me on my back.

The guy with muscles is up high against my chest, between my legs spread wide enough for one to be off over the edge of a single bed, like in a dorm.

My hands are on the shoulders of the guy with muscles. The skinny guy is reaching over him to try and get to me, too. There's an alarm clock and a couple of books on the prop table beside the bed, lots of unused condoms.

An Escort

In the city, I start to lose my taste for everything. I wander around in this state of feeling I need, constantly. I'm going to an office building to meet a man. Sign in once I get there. Do I know what his agency does?

Yes.

Are you gay?

Yes.

But not enough said. What follows is a series of questions. I don't know how tall I am and lie, say what I think I remember from my driver's license. Something like 5′9″.

Oh, so you're tall, he thinks, then asks me how much I weigh.

Again, I take a guess since I don't measure myself like this. Something like 135 I think is almost right.

Tall, skinny, I wonder if I'll be rejected, try to see myself in his eyes. He asks me if I'm a ribcage or abdomen.

Abdomen, I say.

Then he's not so sure, asks me if I know the difference. I laugh a little, sure I know the difference.

His clients go to the best hotels. I'll often have to be able to walk across a lobby and sign in without calling too much attention to myself. Do I think I can handle that?

I wonder how much work I'll get with short blond hair and blue eyes.

Those are the preliminaries.

He says I don't get a second chance, that first impressions are everything, tells me not to be late.

I go for a coffee beforehand, look at myself in the mirror in the restroom. I really only see my face, though. I know he's going to think I look like a little boy.

The coffeehouse starts closing, and it's almost time.

I circle the block, window shop until then.

He tells me that business is slow right now, that I'm more attractive when I smile. Maybe after Labor Day he might have something for me.

He wishes I had a little more of a body, but he encourages me to try other agencies. He'll keep my number, just in case.

The second agency I call is open twenty-four hours. I call around midnight. I get basically the same questions, except the one about whether or not I think I'd be able to sign in at nice hotels. They'll give me an interview. I should bring a picture for the file, and a phone bill to establish residency. I'll actually be filling out an application. The man on the phone gives me an address for a phone booth I should call him from for further directions.

I go to the wrong street, think the place is an apartment complex with wood paneling where a group of small boys are helping an older man do midnight janitorial work, taking out full black garbage bags to a curb. I call again from the pay phone. It's hard to hear what the guy who answers is saying.

He says someone came out to get me. I wasn't there. Where was I?

The guy is mad, claims he didn't say anything about 76th Street. I heard him wrong. Someone else is being interviewed now. I'll have to wait. He'll send someone out again. Later. I wait on the steps in front of a shiny silver building, eye every stranger with possibility, suspicion.

Someone should have been out to get me in twenty minutes.

The agency is located in the basement of a building next door. When the man finally comes out, he leads me past washing machines and dryers, partitions of drywall. Then I have to sit and wait in a black rubber chair next to another empty chair. The interview is going to start in a second. First, can I run an errand for him and his partners? Three people will be interviewing me. Go up to the store and buy drinks. Gatorade for everyone, he lisps.

There are two young, beautiful and thin, light skinned black women waiting in the room with the chairs and phone. The man keeps coming out of a bedroom door he closes behind him. One of the women has a carton of food and eats at a steel desk painted to look like dark varnished wood, in front of a small, fuzzy television that breaks up occasionally, sparks of green dots popping.

One of the women from before has had to leave before making any money, to go home and check on her kids. She explains to the man who seems to be running everything that it's a family emergency. The other woman is still there, wrapped up in a white wool blanket, sleeping on her side on a couch in the room with the desk, television, phone.

The final question of my interview is get hard so they can measure my dick. On my way to the bathroom, I'm scolded for turning on too many wrong lights.

It's different here than with the man I saw earlier in the office building with the elevator, glass doors, interior with nice carpet, what looked like leather couches. He wore a suit. There were magazines spread on a glass and silver table gleaming with a silver tray of miniature cologne samples.

I dropped my pants and took off my shirt, left on my shoes and socks, twirled. He had said something approving before no.

He said if he ever called me back, we'd talk more, about pagers, other fine points.

For the second interview, they are going to eat first, the man whose words I can barely make out and his partners. They offer me food I decline. What's wrong? They joke. Do I think it's poison?

It's past two in the morning. There are four dogs. The partners are another man and one white, older woman. One of the dogs is a pudge with a wrinkled face, silver brown in front of me. Then I'm working myself through my hands, coming back from the bathroom, trying to keep the erection so they can measure, and the dog turns around and puts it's ass in my face. I know I could get harder if one of the men would just kiss me.

I should go back to the bathroom, they tell me, because my erection is all but gone now.

The woman asks me where I'm from, and when I say Georgia,

she says she loves Atlanta. They ask if I brought a picture like they asked, to attach to my application, so when they are flipping through later they'll remember who I am. I offer them my student I.D. from college. It's the only picture I have with me. No, they'll take a Polaroid.

It's snapped of me with no shirt.

My white skin is too pale for the white wall that's the background.

They don't want me standing like that, with my shoulders and arms like that. I don't know how to show myself to my best advantage yet.

I've got a nice swimmer's build, one of them says.

I glow weird in the photo.

Do you kiss? Do you French? Do you know what that means? They ask and tell me it means oral.

Do I do S&M? Domination, submission?

It depends, I say. Then ask how involved it gets.

Sometimes it gets pretty. Would I be all right with some guy peeing on me in the shower?

Can I be a top or a bottom, both?

Do I know what that means?

The guy who is interviewing me, the one back in the room behind the door while the other was looking for me on the street, his name is Chase. I don't want to find him handsome, like I do. He eats take-out lying on the mattress back in the room in sweat pants. Do I do couples? I assume they're a couple. Of course.

They'll call me, and that's it.

Oh, but first we have to think up four or five names for me. This part takes forever. Who do people say I look like? Who do I look like on TV? We finally arrive at Woody, Arthur, Katch.

Those sound like $200 and $300 names, but we really need a $500 one before I go. Think of the names they've been using, they prompt each other, searching for me, helping me look. Think of the boys who I went to school with, the preppy boys, they tell me. Think of something foreign, rich, something Scandinavian, Icelandic, Irish.

I just moved here, but Chase asks me finally if I have any references.

I'm supposed to call back tomorrow, come back tomorrow night.

Turn out the lights on your way out, Chase tells me.

Am I affiliated with the police force?

There will be no one on the train this late at night but drunks and homeless people. Someone will be pissing on the platform, and I will start thinking about how it's romanticizing, really, to call the subway the train.

They Change the Subject

sensory overload

The hotel I am going to is across the street, even higher than most of the other buildings. It goes up into the sky. Before I start, I have a coffee. Soon, it will be time. I won't know if I'm ready until I get over there. Part of my job is to be on time, when they want me up there.

I finish my coffee, walk across the street. I go in the elevator up to the thirty-sixth floor, room twenty-three. There's a cleaning cart outside in the hall. I knock. He opens a door after a moment. I could hear him fumbling behind it. We must shake hands. He says his name is Brian, my first boyfriend. I say my name is Bobby.

Well, he'd like to start with a nude massage, and then we can take it from there. He wears a smell from high school, the same cologne all the boys wore to get the girls they wanted.

Brian wears designer socks. He's from Ohio. I think of my mom's family.

He's just up for the weekend. He just decided to come up for the weekend.

He's a body, a warm body.

Jimmy

He's a nice guy, a regular customer, says the man who arranges the dates. The date has a doorman who asks me if he can help me, what room I'm looking for, my name. I'm someone else today, fucking up, not keeping his mind on his work.

I'm twenty, swimmer's build, etc. He's a big talker. He leads me into the mahogany bedroom of dark wood, after he lets me in. Notice the Indian statues, the cherry wood carvings of dumb things like dolphins, next to a swan, its long neck a different color than in real life. He sits in his chair in the corner of the bedroom, smoking his Pall Malls, a whole pack on the wood table.

He asks me lots of questions, talking over discolored teeth. What did I say my name was again? Where am I from?

Down South isn't a good enough answer for him.

And what did I do last night? Never mind. Where do I live? What did I do today? Why did I come to New York? No answer is noncommittal enough. He'd like a massage, but doesn't take his underwear off yet, so I guess it's all right for me to leave my jeans on, although I do take off my shoes, socks, and T-shirt. He wears designer underwear.

After what must have been the first five minutes, I watch the red digits of the digital clock close to the bed. If I spend the first half of the hour massaging his back, then by the time he flips himself over, it'll be halfway done. I'll only have to be with him thirty minutes. He gets hard, takes his underwear down, opens my jeans. The zipper gives, gold teeth splitting. I watch myself in the glass of a picture frame. It shows how I hold my stomach in. There will always be some boy more willing than me after me.

What are you doing this evening?

We are through, now. I stare at his bookcase, the line of hard-backs standing up by themselves on the ledge.

I might go to a movie. He asks which one.

He's seeing friends, he says, satisfied.

Enjoy the movie, he says.

Thanks, or something. I leave after telling him I hope he enjoys himself, too. He doesn't tip.

mirrors

Elevators in buildings start smelling like them, men. It's also where I prepare myself, while they are taking me up to where I have to go, the right floor. I check myself in all the reflective surfaces inside, after announcing myself to doormen who know I don't live anywhere near there.

Sometimes I can see myself on the ceilings.

I part my hair on the side, just left of center, slick it down with a little spit, then arrive, buzz. A door opens. He notices me just standing there, reaches out to start with shaking my hand, pleased to meet me.

On the way out, I always make sure to say goodbye and thank the doormen, too.

down South

They tell you at all the agencies never to accept food or drinks from a client. They could put something in it. If they ever take you out to dinner, though, and sometimes they might want to, you can have whatever you want. Of course they'll pay. It's safe.

Do you want a drink? Are you sure? You seem kind of nervous. I don't drink.

That's boring. Don't you have any vices? I ask him what he does, and he drinks and smokes, points to a cigarette in his hand, his vodka.

Why don't you take a shower? You look kind of hot, he says.

Would he like me to? Yes. And why don't I shave, while I'm in there, too.

OK. I don't know if I should leave the door open. The curtain is milk-white. I don't know if I'm supposed to dress again after finished with the water, if this is part of the fantasy or not. Like I live here, we're married. Or I'm the son. I use his razor, nicking myself badly, start bleeding down my face. I comb my hair, can still hear him in the other room, ice cubes. Can't find any band-aids, just toilet paper.

I carry my shoes out to the living room where he grins goofily on the couch. He tells me he has two children. He takes me out to get some band-aids. He doesn't want to leave me alone in his house. Going along could all be part of the scenario, too, a trip to the pharmacy for a toothbrush. Maybe I won't have to have sex with him at all. Maybe that's not going to be part of this one.

On the way to the elevator, he tells me he's a direct descendant of Robert E. Lee. He thinks the South is the only place in the States with any real culture. Then he starts in on the Civil War. I smile.

I hear you're from Chicago, he thinks he remembers the agency telling him. They can never keep all us boys straight.

No, I'm from a little town called Macon. Georgia, I white lie.

Macon isn't that little. I've heard of it. I've been through there before.

What did you think? You must do a lot of traveling. Then he wants to know where I go to school, what I study, what I want to be when I grow up. He asks me what Southern writers I like to read. I don't know what makes me say I like Faulkner.

Really? William Faulkner used to read to him as a child. He was a friend of the family. He sang to him when he was still in the crib. Of course he doesn't remember any of this, but that's what they tell him.

His two children are named after Robert E. Lee's kids.

Back at his house, he asks me if I've ever been to Europe. I sit on a footstool across from him. It seems he's lived almost everywhere, asks me if I ever want to go to Asia.

Sure. I'd go anywhere just to see it once.

Well, we should get started. As far back as I can see, there are no pictures on the white walls in a dark room. The bedspread is green and white or blue and white, big canvas stripes. He pushes me where he wants me. I'm a little scared of him now. He wants to take my shirt off at the foot of the bed, so I lift up my arms. He starts undoing my pants, but has problems with the belt. I wait.

I'll let you take your own shoes off, he says.

He pushes me back and rubs all over me. He shoves a fat tongue into my mouth I suck and bite on, can feel the hard pearls of his teeth, the weight of his big brown body naked now. One, two, maybe even three fingers go into me as he arches me roughly up, giving me a tongue to clamp down on.

He asks me if I came.

Yes. Wait here. He goes out closing the door behind him. It's dark on the bed. I sit up and look around. A brass bedside lamp. He comes back, tells me to lie back down, completely covers my body with a mauve-purple bath towel in this light, saturated with hot water. He's going to wipe me off. I can no longer see the clock. He wants to embrace me, spoon me. He wants me to stay all night, keeps touching me. He's almost fighting me to keep me on the bed.

Look, I really have to go. Look, come on. Time's up. I have to get a little rough with him to show him I'm serious.

Did I have fun? Do I want to stay? How much would he have to pay me to stay all night?

I have to go. I can't stay.

How much? How much? He asks again.

As he lets me go, he asks what I'm doing tomorrow night. How about spending the night tomorrow night?

You have to call the agency.

He gives me a seventy-five dollar tip, asking me to please just give him a hand-job before I go.

longer than the last one

He doesn't want to let me go, keeps extending the session. This means I have to call the agency, say I'm staying longer, another half-hour for seventy-five dollars. I don't want the agency to get too worried.

After the first hour, there's a break on the going rate. Three hours soon feel more like four. Four hundred and fifty dollars, plus forty dollars for my cab, there and then away, but first he wants to buy another five minutes for twenty dollars. Can he?

Before it got to that point, he opened the door after I knocked. He was in just his black underwear, likes to talk he told me. He talked while he touched me. He was so hot in that suit, sweating, he explained, he got right into the shower as soon as he got over

115

here, to the hotel. I got to leave my clothes on for a long time with him, while we just talked. He laid over me. I had the feeling I needed to protect myself. He had me start with a condom on my finger going into his ass. I looked up at the light fixture, to try and be uninvolved.

My body is always tense, ready to spring. He did cocaine on the table beside the bed, drank a couple of beers, smoked. He offered me everything. No thanks.

Since high school, college, he's only been with guys from the agency. He only wanted a light massage, what he calls tickling, for me to trail my fingers up and down.

First on his stomach, then on his back.

I'll do you next, he offers.

He's Italian, he tells me. He has five sisters, massages me for an hour. He has me put my jeans back on so he could feel me through them. Next he wanted to see me soft. He wanted me to sit in the chair against the wall. He placed a pillow there between the back of my head and the wall, then went down on me.

Would I mind fucking him? He measured me off, showed me before I started just how much of me he wanted in him, just that far. He put a condom on me and explained he has only just started experimenting with anal sex. He doesn't use any lewd words.

He told me about how he talked all the boys on his basketball team into letting him give them hand-jobs, letting him watch them jerk-off. He told me all the lines he used on them. He lightly stroked fingers on my hand.

Just don't come in my mouth, he said.

He got back into his suit. I could feel his pressed shirt between my legs. He told me about the two times he was caught jerking-off growing up. Then he told me about a friend of his family, some small boy he knows he feels lust for. He doesn't know what to do.

The whole time he left on VH-1. I said I didn't mind, as he fumbled with the remote. He said I have his favorite type of body.

Thanks, I smiled.

He means it. He held my dick, held it hard in his hand. He had to go meet his girlfriend soon, or he would have stayed there all night with me, longer even, he said. He wishes sometimes he could just tell her about me. He said he would remember me later, would remember undressing me, taking off jeans I wear low. He kisses me on my cheek, as I am leaving, after counting out money to me in the chair, just wanted to see me soft, first, before he let me go, since he hadn't seen that yet.

there

He's so young, and he has the same hair color as the boy I was in love with in high school, curled close like a lamb's. His body is thin. He calls me Jim when I tell him my name is Jimmy.

So what do you like to do?

It's pretty much up to you, I say. I'm pretty versatile, I say after he prods me some more. I finally suggest we start with a massage and take it from there. Sounds good. We go into the other room. He has a roommate, but the roommate isn't home. He gets on his stomach and I get on his back on the bed.

To tell you the truth, I'm not often with men, he says. He says he doesn't get to be.

It's a hundred and seventy-five flat, right?

Right. And no, I'm not a cop. He lifts up his shirt, shows me his body. He spreads his fingers out to the sides of my legs, touches me while I work on his trim back. He wants to fuck me, goes to look in the bathroom for some lube he says he has.

Can't find it. I could fuck him. Sure. Time's almost up.

Play with my ass, he says. He wants to kiss a lot. That always makes it feel more real. He feels bad because he didn't get me off.

It doesn't matter, I say.

He wants to give me a hug before I go, after we talk a little.

turned off

The oldest guy I've ever been with has a porno he puts in and wants me to watch while he does cocaine. He offers the drugs to me and says that's what he wants to see tonight, what's on the TV. I pretend to be absorbed, waiting in a chair in front of the porno for the other boy coming from the agency to join me.

He's late, fem. But he wants to be the one to fuck me, when he finally arrives. Fine. I think about just leaving, but instead I kiss the boy who makes the old man undress, plays with him a little before getting up on the bed with me as the man takes my seat in front of the TV.

We are up on our knees, cheek to cheek facing the old man, then pecking, little pecking pecks. I'm just following the other boy who follows the TV, who thinks we are show boys or something, peep-show performers, Siamese twins. I am fucking nauseated.

The old man comes over and rubs my nipples. The boy fucks me for about an hour after he left me alone with the old man some more, ran out for some condoms. I try to keep my eyes closed the whole time. The TV is still on. The movie rolls. We fuck along with the boys fucking on the screen.

The old man tells me he thinks the boys are cute, that me and the boy are cute, too. We make a cute couple, he says. The old man says the men in the porno are good actors. My partner wants to leave the TV on. I know I'm going to be sore all day tomorrow, up inside of me. The feeling won't go away, even if I don't think about it. I will have to live with it, even though I don't suck the old man, don't even touch him. I just want to get out of there, close my eyes. After the way he fucks me, I let my partner do the rest of the work we are getting paid to perform on the old man.

Disney

He expects me to talk. We talk for a little while. He just got back from vacation. Really? I don't ask what he does for a living, so he fills an awkward silence by telling me all the places he could one day live. He just got offered some job. We talk a little about my job. He thinks it's best if you make up your mind to only do it for a little while.

But most people get sucked in, I add for him. It's such good money, so fast. It requires so little time. Well, let's go upstairs, where he asks me if I want to pick out some music. Then he wants me to come over onto the bed. I don't even have to undress all the way. I just lie there like a dead fish, letting him feel the contours of my face, cheekbones, lips, and areas under my eyes. I shut. Now there's nothing to focus on but the smell of his breath. I don't want to kiss him. He keeps kissing around my lips, to the side of my lips, the side of my face I keep turning.

He takes down my pants. I'm glad I'm hard. Pulls up my shirt.

My shoes get kicked off, followed by his. He opens his own pants. I only have to touch him once the whole time. He plays with me, spanks me lightly swatting at my ass. When he comes on my leg, he exclaims a low wow, wow.

That was quite excellent, he says later while giving me my money, asking how much I get to keep, how much goes to the agency. Here, take his phone number, in case I ever want to call him myself, keep all of the money. He is usually home weekends and nights.

subservient

Only a psychiatrist would use such a word in bed, actually articulate it. I've been warned by the agency that this one might send me away. If he does, don't take it personally, but he doesn't. He's just picky. He has a nice dog and a messy bedroom. We do it in the living room on a couch that folds out, after he brings in more pillows and blankets. He wants me to take a shower, take my time, brings in a robe for me to wrap up in after. Dove soap. He likes to rim a guy, but he doesn't like dirty butts.

Are you nervous?

No. He's projecting. He's a little nervous.

His office is right up the street.

He wears white briefs with his white button-up shirt, open. I'm glad he likes me on whatever level. He positions a mirror so he can watch me on his face, arch my back. He wants me to talk to him, talk dirty. What do I think of him eating out my butt? He thinks it's hot, so hot. He'd like to do it to me while someone else watched. Then he asks me if my older brother ever did this to me.

Yeah.

You have an older brother? I'm guessing he does, too. Between his questions, he tongues.

It started when I was thirteen.

Did you do other things together? It was just your little secret?

Yeah. I guess.

repeat

There is always that moment where I give up, to get it over with, just have to relax completely into it. He's kissing me. Just let him look at me, my neck, turn my head, kiss the sides of my mouth. He pushes his tongue in. It's quieter when he turns the stereo up.

Holiday Inn

He's from Connecticut, here on business. Only here for a few days, meeting friends tonight. Since I can't see a clock in the hotel room, I keep track of time by half-hour shows on TV. There's *Oprah,* then some human interest story on the news about a dog, followed by a court show.

I rub his freckled back with baby oil. He says that's the best rubbing he's had in a long time, turns over. I moan, but his dry tongue is like scales. He won't stop trying to kiss me. He asks me if I like him slapping me. He doesn't come.

Yes.

I slide all over him. Then dress to take the elevator down to the street.

5:25 appointment

I sleep with my first Asian in the most expensive hotel I've ever been to. Elevators are all glass sides. You watch the floor, as you shoot up, disappear under you. He's just come back from a play on Broadway, wastes no time getting naked.

He wants me on top of him, so I start smelling him like a dog for some reason.

You smell good, he says, breaking into my pants while I stare down at his dark flesh of testicles. He asks me to lick them, tells me my dick is huge. He says it feels so good, coos another language as he's coming in the room.

I spit on the carpeted floor when he goes off to the bathroom to wash, rub my tongue on the linen on the bed, trying to find a dry spot. He gives me a one hundred and twenty-five dollar tip for an hour that took ten minutes.

two hours

We're using my pimp's apartment for this one, so I have to get there fifteen minutes early. My pimp folds out the couch, assures me the sheets were changed recently. The man coming weighs two hundred and ten pounds, he prepares. He's a nice guy. He turns on the radio and leaves, telling me I'm supposed to go to the door without any shoes or socks on to meet the guy.

Once he gets there, he's full of commands, clumsily undresses me. He wants to leave the light on, wants me to come on his chest in the first fifteen minutes.

Only an hour and forty-five more minutes to go. Can he come on my chest? Sure. The blinds are open. He says something about the eyes and seeing into the soul, keeps telling me to open them. He wants me to stare right into his eyes. I don't want to look at him. He says he's blind as a bat without his glasses. He tells me I should be a model, that I've got a great body, that he likes my dick. Of course. He asks if I've been told this before.

I lie and say I'm twenty.

Do your parents know you're gay? I've been told he's a momma's boy, that he saves up all his money for this, something like me, once a month. I lie there with my eyes closed and nod. Yeah. He likes young boys. Give him my hand, do this. Get on top of him, press down on his chest.

He brought some condoms. I lay there and try to listen to the radio in the background. Do I have a boyfriend? How much do I weigh? I try to fuck him like he wants me to, but can't. I start blacking out, dreaming, heavy, I'm on my back so long. He wants me to have a second orgasm, so I try to imagine someone I love on top of me.

I keep concentrating on a mirage of blue eyes while the guy I'm with tells me some story about seducing a chemistry teacher in lab. He had a key to the lab, undressed the teacher there. It went on for three or four years.

Really? They did it in the teacher's basement apartment and over at his parents' house.

Really?

The mattress is so thin, he has a lot of trouble getting up out of the bed. He wants me to come again.

How old was your oldest customer ever?

Sixty, I guess.

Old enough to be your grandfather, huh?

Yeah.

He wants me to guess his age.

Thirty.

No, he's thirty-one.

Where are you from?

Virginia. I wipe off with a towel from the bathroom, onto the pink roses. Time's up.

Hand him his glasses, his watch from the table.

Before he goes he says I'm the type of guy he'd like to take home to his mother.

Carlyle

I'm called to go to a hotel I think I know, think maybe I've been to before with an ex-boyfriend, a nice hotel. But I'm not going to meet anyone I know.

There are quick pleasantries. He'll pay extra if we go past the hour, majored in economics. I wonder if he has a wife and family back home in Washington, what I'm doing to them. Afterwards, I want to wash my mouth out with soap. I feel like I should apologize for coming. He made a mess of me. He offers to let me take a quick shower before I go. There's expensive yellow soap wrapped in plastic sealed with the hotel's monogram, a stack of twenties on the dresser waiting for me when I get out.

Mexican

He's waiting for me to make all the moves, says in his broken English he wants me to seduce him. OK. He's cute, young, mostly sweet.

What do you want to do?

What do you do?

It depends, it's up to you.

No, it's up to you.

I can see already my usual routine is not going to work. He doesn't seem too keen on the idea of a massage, suspects me, wants me to know right away that's not all he's here for, missing the subtext.

OK. Does he want the TV on? He says it's up to me.

Really, I want to say, it isn't. You're the one paying for this.

But maybe he wants to pretend we just happened to meet and end up here.

Do you want the lights on? It's up to me.

I leave the TV on.

He says he does anything but get fucked. I tell him don't be nervous, I'm not going to fuck him if he doesn't want to be fucked. We go through motions like we are doing it even though we aren't, his legs wrapped around me. I make like ramming into him.

tall

He starts touching, touching my hands. Can he offer me anything to drink?

He turns my hands around and over in his, laughs off my tattoo.

I can taste his breath, the entire bottle of white wine he's already drunk. Follow him into the bedroom, passing another room with a child's drawing taped to a closed door.

Guess he's married, doesn't say anything when I say he has a big place. The bed is large, so large. He keeps saying oh yes, oh yes, that's great, as I grit my teeth into his shoulder, his wife away. He asks me what the hottest thing I like is, doesn't believe me when I say I've already come. Lick him some more.

hate

He's young, so I'm a little more concerned about pleasing him. The TV is on football.

I sit on top of a low dresser in the hotel room, while he sits in a chair.

Why don't you get comfortable, he dares me.

I take my shoes, socks, and shirt off. Looks like he doesn't like me. His eyes are red, starts touching the lump in his pants, then moves over to the swell that starts to gather in mine, touches one of my nipples. I keep trying to get around the inevitable blow job, but just my hands on his thick thighs mean nothing to him. He gets brave enough to push me back on the bed and kiss me a little, seems slightly Southern, likes my face more underneath the pillow. From that point on, I'm just a body, try to move the pillow off, but he puts it back, cranks two or three fingers harshly into me, puts me in a better position to be fucked from.

I can't let you fuck me without a condom.

Oh, yeah. That's right. He must have forgot.

He manages to bruise me somewhat.

This hotel has come to expect me. They take me up in the elevator without even asking what floor. He quickly rips the rubber off, while I keep moving around under the pillow. Then I feel him fall on me in splashes of hot. He walks off to the shower.

Now I avoid looking at him until I can get out of there.

I sit on the floor, put back on my shoes. Here man, or something like that, he throws money at me.

darker

The quality of the tape is poor, not very clear. The movie's been dubbed. It's not an American porno. Guys aren't as assembly-line.

He wants me to lie down on the light brown, tan rug, asks me if I get fucked.

Sometimes.

Now? He says he isn't that big, so it shouldn't hurt too much. Thankfully he wants me on my stomach. That way I don't have to look at him. His apartment is barely furnished but for the TV in front of the couch. He uses his spit to lubricate. He wants to know if I'm coming. He wants me to come on him. I accidentally get it all over his face.

Washing up, only his black toothbrush is in the bathroom. There's nothing even to dry off with. I just put my clothes back on wet, and he asks if I'm leaving.

Yeah.

Eighteen to twenty-five, he says those are the best years of life.

It's my birthday. I don't tell anyone. It takes me forever to get back home.

hunger

He says handing me the money that god, there are people who can't even eat in this world, and here we are doing this.

He's right. I'm going to eat good tonight. When he comes back in November, he wants to know if he can just ask for me by name at the agency.

6 a m

He had a stressful day, meeting after meeting. Started as soon as he got here. He's from Cincinnati. He leaves first thing in the morning.

We move to where the two king-sized beds are, a view of the city spread out before us.

Let's not get too comfortable, he says when I lay back on the bed.

He made me go at him so long, I don't even want to touch the condom when I finally pull out of him. The next day I can still smell him in my hair.

the same old questions

When he finally opens the door, I go in and say his name.

Bob, it's Bobby.

I estimate answers to his detailed questions. He starts to hold my hand, and I close my eyes. Can't see myself there with him. Wonder how little I can get away with giving him. He pats an area next to him on the bed. Join him. There are a lot of scabs, on his hands and legs. He blows me while I lie back on the bed. He watches himself in the mirror undressing me. I try to act shy and ashamed to get him really hot.

Oh, Bobby, that hurts. That hurts. Lower Bobby.

He is on his knees and I can barely get inside. Stay right there, Bobby. He comes on the bedspread.

I leave him there with something isolated in his eyes.

He seems like he can't believe I'm going now, looks slightly dejected, asks me to tickle his back for a little, says all I really have is my health.

short

He used to be a teacher. Now he's a salesman. He likes to kiss and hug, be nice to people, have people be nice to him, so kiss him.

Are you tired?

No. Why?

Because your eyes keep closing.

I try to keep them open.

How come you don't wear any underwear?

More clothes to take off.

Billy isn't really your name, is it?

nice house

There's a courtyard, a stone walkway to the door, a garden of green shrubbery. He has a big screen TV, the biggest I've ever seen.

He says he's relatively inexperienced. I say don't worry.

He says for this it doesn't matter, but in real life, you need to look people in the eyes, that it makes all the difference in business.

books

Have you ever met any weirdoes?

No.

Any really ugly men?

One or two.

Really obese ones?

One or two.

How many guys work for the agency?

I don't know. Five?

What do you think people who call are asking for when they get you?

I don't know.

What are you reading?

Lolita. I'm looking for my shirt. He only reads nonfiction. Oh.

More water?

No thanks.

Are any of your clients celebrities? Do you ever get to travel with any of your clients?

No.

Do you have a boyfriend? He guesses it would be pretty hard.

I have one, I lie.

prep

I come home to a message to call Todd, who is really Jim. We've worked out this code so my roommates will not have to know what I do for a living. I've started dressing differently, for a new agency. They like a more clean-cut look, no jeans, no tennis shoes. I shave, and I part my hair. Put on khakis and a periwinkle shirt that buttons up, an outfit I'd originally bought to do temp work in. At least it's being used.

I pull over the shirt the nicest sweater I own, a gift from the last one I loved.

It doesn't feel right. He is still often in my thoughts.

I think if only I hadn't let myself do this.

I'm told I look like a boarding school boy. I say that's the point, my new look. Another one of my roommates asks how I pay rent. I'm elusive and say my checks.

The old agency paged and expected me to be wherever within an hour. The new agency calls to ask if I'll be around tonight. Call later to say there'll be a call later to confirm. Call later to confirm, give me all the information.

10pm

The woman working the phones tells me to look Ralph Lauren or Gap. The man who hired me, Jim, said Banana Republic. Be exactly on time. I'm given the man's name to give to the doorman who will give me the apartment number of a gorgeous place on Park. The man will want to talk about sports or politics, two subjects I'm completely worthless in, ask if I give good massages. We always say we do. He tips anywhere from twenty to one hundred dollars. There's always the mind game of if I could make him like me more, I could possibly make more money, by maybe making him think something really happened. I wasn't just being merely cooperative.

Call when I get there. I don't have to call when done, just report back to the woman who takes the calls and give her the agency's cut.

He'll want to fuck me, but that should only take about five minutes.

here

Hockey. I lie and say it's probably my favorite sport.

Why?

The skates make it graceful.

He has finished all his Christmas shopping. All but one present. He took a week off work to do it. What about me? Have I done my Christmas shopping?

Then, do I like to give massages?

I follow him through huge rooms that lead to the bedroom. There's even room for a massage table. That's how much he likes massages.

Nothing touches a surface directly. Drinks in glasses are on napkins. Bring your drink. He warns about staying on the towel, once we move from the massage table to bed. He lays down a monogrammed towel, for when I step out of the shower. Make sure to step out onto the towel.

massage

He tells me to fold my clothes up in that chair there. My mind starts to drift out the window and over the skyline. This scene is not my home.

He grabs me, asks if he should turn over on the table. Wow. He tells me I'm blessed.

Yeah.

He wants to fuck me no matter how much it hurts, so I lay there where he's not satisfied until he comes. I stay facedown on the towel.

He asks me if I have a boyfriend, if my boyfriend and I fuck each other.

He gives me a big tip. He likes me. The woman at the agency won't believe me when I tell her how much. The woman at the agency thinks I look like someone I'm not.

entrance

He hides me while the elevator is brought up. Then sneaks me out the door, into the hall, making sure first none of his neighbors are around.

In the lobby, I walk past a couple who live in the building, my hair still wet.

evening plans

I call a number when Jim can't offer me enough work, to set up my own dates, leave my voice with all my descriptions.

I've been staying in a friend's apartment, waiting for the pager to go off. It does, twice, so I return the two calls and now have something to do.

overdressed

It's a nice hotel. I'm almost afraid to go in. I get off the elevator on the wrong floor, get back in, go up some more.

Luckily he doesn't ask my name. I don't know what I'd say.

He doesn't try to make conversation. Good. I sit on the bed. He sucks me. That's all, really. He's undemanding. He strokes me lightly, once or twice, bracing my lower back with a hand. Pays me up front.

His dark brown hair is conservatively cut. In front of me on the bed, he goes between standing up and crouching down on one knee, seems afraid to get too close, never gets on the bed.

We redress in silence. On the TV is a show about a psychiatrist.

Is it cold outside? It felt like it was going to get colder.

over the phone

He wants to know if I look like anybody. Do I look like any celebrity? Not that I can think of, right off hand, I say. He asks me how I wear my hair, how long it is. There's no agency to tell me what his tastes will be.

Between long and short.

He sees.

Between curly and straight.

He sees.

I tell him I'll be there within the hour.

He asks again, am I sure I'm attractive?

business

He starts undressing as soon as I come in. I massage him in front of the TV. I fade in and out of half-touching him. It's scary how quiet he is. *Ellen* is on Lifetime. I make a go at him to try and get it over with, but he moves my hand away.

On the bedside table are two white hand towels. On the nightstand there is a wedding picture. The phone rings once. The machine picks up. He looks like he wants me to say something, so I hug him goodbye.

Standing up, he is shorter than me. Outside I count the wad of bills he gives me.

baby doll

He plays with my hip sockets, as if my joints could easily be snapped out of place, legs removed, and then put back.

He tells me I'm a lovely young man.

His body is a huge frame. He runs a butler service.

He was working Christmas day. He'll be working New Year's Eve.

What did I do for Christmas? Do I have plans for New Year's Eve? I'm trying to figure out who he looks like, realize it's Sean

Connery, so he's not exactly repulsive. He doesn't seem as depressed as the last one, asks me what happened to my Southern accent, asks me what I studied in school. He laughs when I say English.

He smoothes down my now mussed hair. He puts his hand down into the front pockets of my coat, pulls out a cartoon pocket mirror I've got in one. A present.

street

There are awkward spaces of quiet between us to fill in the car, during the ride to his place. He picks me up in his brand new utility vehicle. He seemed normal enough.

So how long have you been doing this?

About three months. I reassure him it's not bad.

We strip down in the bedroom. I just want to make love to someone. We go through the motions of the massage. There are pictures of kids. He moves me through lots of positions. He waits to, wants to, see me come before he lets go. Seems surprised by how much I kiss.

At first it's like it's real, so I force myself to get more indirect and sloppy.

He doesn't tip me, doesn't ask how he can see me again.

shave

The weird thing is I've started wanting to go.

When one of them calls too late one night, he's sure it's too late. He just wanted to check-in with me. I say it's not too late. I say it's never too late, that I'll come.

buzz

Do I want something to drink?

Water.

Do I mind if he smokes?

No.

He says I'm smart, for not smoking. He's in advertising.

Where do I live? Where am I coming from? What train do I take? What street do I live on? Where do I work? What street?

How much do I work? Is he asking me too many questions?

I hadn't quite prepared my stories before getting there, so I end up letting a lot of truth slip. I ask him to quit asking questions. He just wants to make me more comfortable, says I seem nervous. He doesn't stop talking in bed, wants to know if my other clients ask me to skip the body massage. He says I feel fabulous, fabulous.

Though he's not even hard, he goes through the motions of fucking me, simulating entering, just pounding his body up against mine.

spring

There was no air moving in the room, and so the air was still and hot and sticky. He was sweating, almost the largest man I'd ever slept with. His hair felt greasy, but it's just all the sweat.

The sheets on his bed were pink. The art print on the wall had one word I read as alone. He told me to look at him. He told me that he loved my hair. That hurts me, when he plays with it.

I don't want his tongue in my mouth, but he eventually forces it in. I don't want to lie on top of him, but he wants me there. I don't want to touch him, to know him at all, but do. I watch him take my clothes off, then just close my eyes. I keep them that way for almost a whole hour.

His thumb pokes one of my eyes, at one point, and I think I would welcome violence.

Close, there is an elementary school, and the kids are playing at recess. I can hear them, screaming, yelling, playing. By the end of the hour, their voices have receded.

His house is so dirty he walks throughout clutter everywhere in slippers. He keeps trying to hold onto me. I try to think about other things. He trails his fingers up and down my back. There was some sort of breathing machine, oxygen, medicine, in a tube on the bedside table, on the other side of the bed. There's a porno tape on the table I can't quite make out. It looks like there is a girl on the cover.

I have to show him I am leaving now.

Too bad. My clothes and skin were dirty. He ran his hands through my hair so many times. The bathroom was disgusting. I wanted to spit, to throw up this, as I was choked on his tongue. He wouldn't keep it out of my mouth, poking it in. I pretended I was in an Eternity ad, that he was my father. It was just my dad's chest I lied across. There was no other implication. I was young, too young. That's all there was to it. I couldn't believe this was me, there. It didn't feel like me. Nothing I tried to do to make this go away, faster this time, seemed to work. I struggled with him. The hour was another hour, a lifetime.

His bathroom tiles were a black scum. I went in there for air.

He said he'd be calling me again, soon.

He kept shoving my face up under his armpit.

The sun kept coming through the window, while he rubbed sweat off on me. I was breathing in gulps now from my mouth,

137

trying not to take in anything through my nose. I pretended I was just a figure in this group photograph. I thought of raging through this space, like I felt like he was violating me, not playing by whatever rules I thought there might have been, smashing his things cluttered all around, that he obviously cared about, turning over the stuffed dressers, biting him like I'd been cornered, one that must guard whatever it was I'd pawed randomly through the world with, turn this so far away from any sweetness it could never be, but at the most basic level should.

An Attempt

It takes us a good two hours to get there.

We have a dog with us named Mouse, a she. She sits up calmly in the backseat until we get far enough out to see horses, a poor cow, tame deer, and other dogs. Then she starts barking, standing up in the backseat, climbing into the front, her tail wagging.

We have our directions printed out, and we have been telling each other stories.

He wanted to just take me away this weekend from everything.

I don't believe there's anything inherently, biologically in me that makes me this way.

It's what I've been exposed to.

I think it's in anyone to do and like, eventually, brushing against his hand on the gear-shift, on accident.

The dog barks excitedly against the car's glass windows, at what she saw beyond them.

Then we are there.

Further into the fold of trees just barely holding leaves the dead colors of scarlet, orange, yellow, cold. Past an in-ground pool in one of the sprawling lawns, filled not with chlorine, but some unswimmable water. Green mosses float on top and scraps of white petals, gold leaves, what may even be lily pads. We park on a deserted drive.

Near here he grew up. I've never been around these parts before. I feel a little guilty for having come out here this weekend. I look around the grounds and indoors. It still feels familiar, still. It's been forever since I've touched someone like him, someone I really wanted to be together with. It's been a long time since.

This weekend, he just wanted my company. I'm to remember that. I'm not to expect, to need too much. I've thought before I would be anything a man might want me to be. We are just being near each other this weekend.

We go through all the rooms, so he can show me where every-thing is, and I leave him somewhat to himself, while the dog runs around free outside. We can hear her barking at birds.

I don't know if he knows what I mean when I say I once thought in order to be kept protected, I'd have to learn how to be stronger than some things. Something made me feel that I needed to be protected, that I wasn't being.

I have to talk this way, because I don't want to scare him away.

There is an upstairs, lots of bedrooms. He is young. He's just started driving. He doesn't have anything to prove to me.

I bring out my books, and I can hear him in the house down-stairs, moving his chair back. There was a letter he wanted to write.

Later, when he's done, we'll go for a walk along the reservoir, before it gets too dark, take the dog out for a walk.

Our faces are blown cold, but we are talking. I think we are all born in a way that's been taken advantage of. We are telling each other stories. There is nothing we can't try to understand about each other. We come from the same background. We understand each other.

Yes, he guesses, similar backgrounds. How did we get here? Where have we been before this moment? We are shivering, the two of us, as the sun begins setting. We might love each other. But we might not touch. He's still young, and he's not sure he's ready for that.

There's something in our backgrounds that might make us more emotionally open, more emotionally ready.

In the field, so many things are getting blue in the distance. Of course, I don't really know what he feels, just because we've been exposed to the same things.

He imagines we feel similar.

There are things I feel I will have to tell him if I'm going to begin to really communicate with him. We must come from a real place. He's scared to just look at me. But I think I want to tell at least one person everything. I want to tell him.

Why when I tell him a story do I feel like there are things it's more important for him to know?

He forgot to bring a coat. He's cold, and I want to give him mine to wrap up in. What will I wear? He has on a warm hat, lined with fur. He'll be fine. But he says we should be getting back. We should take the dog back. We should call it a night.

The next day back in the yard, he throws a stick for the dog.

I can't speak for most men. I don't feel a part of them.

Even the ones like us?

Yes, the ones who feel similar to us.

The dog fetches and then follows me around the house with the stick in her mouth. There are woods all around us. You could just barely hear the highway. Tangible, familiar, it made me think of all the yards there could have been once, homes we both could have one day had, when all I wanted once was to not have to go away, to know how long I was going to stay.

We'd be there for three days. Even this, I felt, could promise something.

What could I give him in the exchange of one weekend?

We had to learn codes that would change once we separated.

In another room across the hall, he is sleeping in the bed. In all this remoteness, what would seem closer, what would hang in the air would be a certain acceptance of our situations.

This is where and how it could all end, if I let it become futile to fight to get more.

With him, it could be like beginning all over again.

Here comes the dog, bounding after another stick, and we went in.

He and I cooked a simple dinner. It was something he might have made for just himself, but tonight, I was there. Tonight, counting the dog, there were three of us. There's a magazine on the table and we know everyone's name in it. Or we are expected to know, supposed to know.

I am telling him one of my stories. He is asking. We'd save some for tomorrow.

I sleep under one white blanket, under a single skylight above the bed. What of this weekend, understanding, would be lost, in trying to put it into words, words that would only try to make it like other weekends.

The sky is filled with stars, constellations. Once we memorized alignment, to help show us the way. Still, sometimes, I would dream of that.

You can't make some dreams go away. In the dreams, well enough would be to touch and still be touched, to make a first, a pure move, to feel something new yet certain, familiar, to feel some grounding.

I've enjoyed this weekend because I can't put into words, yet, what we wanted from each other. We were still exploring each other. We are driving back from the heart of the town, where we went for breakfast. Mouse was staying in the yard. Did we know how to be men, if we wanted to? What did that mean? Why doesn't that ever change? Are we changing it, being together like this? We had to swerve on the highway, right before the turn for the road up to the house, into a lane away from the body crushed there.

I could see where the lower paws should have been. I knew who it was. The head mostly intact, still attached, the body ripe and open.

It was winter and there were clouds coming off her still warm.

He circled around the car, parked a little ways down on the side of the road, while other cars continued their racing over. When I was young, I'd said this was who I was because I didn't want there to have to be any more question. There are some things I can't pretend to know. These words I had just now been saying in the car were still echoing in me.

I stood there with his arms around me, crying. It was his dog. We had to keep moving. He got a box out of the trunk, a blanket.

I tried to block the traffic, to get the cars to go around, as he tried to pick her up.

After he got the rest of her in the box, he put his arms around me.

He shut the trunk, and we drove back to the house silent.

I'll try to help him bury her in the box, in the shade of hedge.

Under a rubber tree, outside in the yard where we'll spend most of the day tomorrow, we dig a hole, break up the ground, shovel out with our hands roots and rocks, trying to get down deep enough to place the remains safely.

I don't necessarily have the same values as the people I sleep with. The first time I went to bed with a man, the first time I'd said yes, I'd try this, with him, with a man, I remember not particularly wanting to do it, until he'd suggested it, until he'd asked me, and I thought if I could do it, that would mean something, prove something.

I split open a large area of my right hand, on one of the roots in the ground.

It was like playing with boys, digging again, boys who know what to do, what should be done, knew something I didn't yet know how to do, called me things.

In acting as such, I had believed them.

I had to turn away and walk off a bit to keep from breaking into a run.

He breathes in big gulps from his mouth, finishing the job of the burying.

We weren't going to just leave her there. We were going to carry her deep inside us.

Her smell will come up against all the windows of the house that night, reminding us all of things we can't name.

I hadn't told myself yet what it was. In the morning, outside, he placed a log over where we'd made the hole last night, a piece of a broken tree. That night, there was the moon again already, scarring the sky, showing us there was another body out there. We had to be leaving soon.

I was going to open my mouth, as the two of us were getting back home.

How could I not become this, when they where looking at me this way, when they were coming onto me, their desire stronger than mine. They believed they knew. I'd begun to believe them.

I was trying to tell him so many things in such little time as we were still allotted, without destroying still tentative things. These were things I didn't think I'd had the words for, ever, ways I'd just felt, reacted, why I'd thought I had to become this person who I'd thought I might have always already been.

It had always been lying under us, waiting to lure us wherever we'd go.

I was trying to put it into some sort of words for him, how sorry I was. I wanted to say something that would mean something. I kept searching for the most immediate way to try and make him understand where I was coming from, that there was somewhere else I wanted to be with him, but he wants to know why I believe he would be any different.

Look at the sky. The sky was incredible tonight. He couldn't remember the last time he'd ever seen a sky like that. Look at the moon.

It's like I escaped into my sexuality.

I could have pointed out to him the way we kept missing the bridge, but I didn't. We were driving back. He must know a

145

different way. He could have been doing it purposefully, to elongate our three days. Just his presence comforts.

It's never been over.